EVERYONE KEEPS SECRETS

FACADES CRUMBLE

By
Katherine Greyson

Facades Crumble

Katherine-Greyson.com

Books in order in the series:

Looking for a high-octane mystery thriller?
Be sure to check out bestselling author
Christopher Greyson's books.

Table of Contents

Facades Crumble

<u>CHAPTER ONE</u>

His Past, Her Future

Robert Kendall
Present Day

Evil men know one thing—under the cover of darkness—it's easier to hide your crimes.

Police Chief Kendall sat in the cruiser deep in the woods with Detective Ken Frisco. The night enveloped the car in a murky black.

"How'd you come across this?" Frisco nodded out the windshield.

"Vera Miles."

"The widow who was married to old John at the gas station?"

"Yeah." Robert pointed in the direction of her farm. "She phoned in a report of odd fumes coming from the canyon. I had a hunch, so I drove here in civilian clothes and an unmarked car out to the old mining road that ran behind her property. When I rolled down the window and smelt rotten eggs mixed with cat urine, I knew what I'd found."

"Meth lab."

Robert nodded.

Detective Frisco took another sip of his coffee trying to stay awake. "Do we know how many guns?"

"No."

"What time does the perp usually show up?"

"Two am. After the bars close." Robert checked his watch.

"Seems like all my police work runs into the night shift." Frisco leaned back in the seat.

Robert rubbed his brow fighting to keep his eyes open, and sharp.

"Doesn't bother me. I've got no one at home waiting for me. But you do." Detective Frisco glanced at Robert. "We have plenty of manpower. No need for you to be here, Chief."

Robert didn't answer. He knew his officers could handle it, but he was never one to put his men in harm's way while he slept in a warm bed.

As they sat in silence, an owl hooted cutting the tension that ran thick through the heavy air of the night. The pale moon retreated behind a bank of clouds.

"How are those daughters of yours?" Detective Frisco stretched out his body. "Your eldest is in high school now, right?"

Robert nodded. "Yeah. She's a junior."

Frisco snickered.

Robert gave him a sharp, sideways glare.

"Sorry Chief." He straightened up. "I was just picturing a boy's terrified face— when your daughter brings him home to meet you for the first time."

Robert fought back a chuckle, and then cleared his throat. The fear his daughter was growing-up filled him with more dread than tonight's raid.

Frisco, appearing bored, looked around and sniffed. "I like this cruiser. It still has that new car smell."

The scent jogged Robert's memory. He gripped the taut, leather steering wheel and thought back to that innocent time in his daughter's life before her mother had passed away. Ten years. It had flown by.

He wondered if he'd prepared his daughter enough for the harsh realities of this world? And if something were to happen to him tonight, would she know how hard he'd tried to protect her and do the right thing? He rubbed at his chest remembering his mistakes from the past. He knew how much they hurt his daughter. He wondered if she could ever forgive him for that.

Chatter over the police radio broke him from his thoughts. A car was approaching. The men checked their sidearms as they prepared for what was coming.

"Well." Frisco adjusted his bulletproof vest. "Here we go."

"Yeah."

Unexpectedly, the beam from a motorcycle's headlight came flying up the dirt road behind them. Frisco jumped in his seat. "Who the hell is that?" The officers rushed out of the cruiser, weapons drawn, just as the sound of gunshots echoed through the canyon.

CHAPTER TWO

Some Hurts Never Heal

Simplicity Kendall
Ten Years Ago

I slid into the back seat and ran my fingertips along the brand-new velvet upholstery as I inhaled the scent of new car that floated in the air. "This is neat, Mom." I bounced on the seat. "Is this what Dad bought you for a present?"

"Not just for me, Simplicity. It's for you too."

I opened up the pocket behind the passenger seat. "I can stuff tons of Barbie doll clothes in here."

My mom smiled.

The old grey haired salesman, who sat in front of me, pointed out the car's other flashy, new features. "Is this your first new automobile, Mrs. Kendall?"

"Yes." She beamed. "My husband wanted to buy a reliable car for us. He didn't like me driving around in my old Chevette anymore."

The car salesman nodded. I put my elbows on top of the seats and leaned in between them. "I liked the old car. It had a cool hole down there," I pointed below my Mom's feet. "You could put your feet on the ground and push it down the hill, just like Fred Flintstone's car."

The man appeared shocked.

My mom blushed. "My husband had our mechanic weld a piece of metal underneath to try and fix it. It was an old, rusted car."

He smiled and nodded.

"I bought it before I got married. I was a social worker. I didn't have much money then."

He smiled warmly. "Well this car has all the latest in safety features. To keep the little ones safe." He nodded toward me.

I popped my head in between them again. "Oh, that's good, 'cause my mom's pregnant."

Her face turned white. She flipped down the rearview mirror and glared at me. "That was supposed to be our little family secret, remember?"

"Oh, yeah . . . I forgot."

She anxiously glanced over at the salesman.

He winked. "I didn't hear a thing, Mrs. Kendall."

"Oh good. Thank you for not letting anyone else know." She smiled sweetly. "I'm only a couple months along, and they say not to tell anyone until the second trimester." He nodded and then, without further comment, went to show her how the radio worked.

My parents had been trying to have another baby for years. They talked about it a lot. At night I would sneak over to my hiding spot behind the stairs and listen to them. When my got pregnant before something happened and no baby came. I never really understood where the babies went—like, did the stork mess up the delivery or something? Whatever it was, I knew it wasn't good. My mom usually ended up crying and my dad would try to make her feel better.

I begged them for a little sister, but my parents said they didn't get to choose. I was confused how it worked. I wondered if there was a way I could get word to the stork and tell him what kind of baby I wanted. Maybe I could write a letter and send it to him, like Santa.

After Mom and the salesman finished, they let me pick out a lollipop from this big jar in the office. Then my mom and I got back into our new car and drove home.

"Mom?"

"Yes, Simplicity?"

"Do you think we could celebrate with ice cream tonight?"

"Is that what you want to do?"

"Uh-huh." I nodded.

"Okay, but I have to check with your father first."

"Great!" I crunched through to the gum at the center of the lollipop—my favorite part.

"When he gets home you need to give him lots of hugs. And tell him how proud we are of him."

"Yes, Mom." She was always reminding me to encourage my dad. "It's because of his new promotion at the station that we can afford this car."

"Should I make him a card?" Just then, my mom's phone rang. I smiled hearing my dad's special ringtone.

"Hi, honey. Yes, we picked up the car. Thank you so much."

As she talked, I played with the neat button that made my window go up and down.

"We need to go where?"

I watched her and hoped "where" was Friendly's. I was dying for a hot fudge sundae.

"Are you sure?" She pinched her lips together.

"Okay." She nodded. "We'll meet you there." Slowly, she put the phone down.

"Where are we going?" I grabbed the cool handle that hung above my window and started pulling, doing little chin-ups.

"We have to meet Daddy at the doctor's office."

"Weren't we there yesterday?"

She gripped the steering wheel tighter. "Yes."

"Are you okay, Mom?"

She nodded, but the way she looked, kinda' worried me.

As we pulled into the parking lot of the Doctor's office, I saw my dad. He was so handsome with his dark hair and green eyes. He stood tall and in charge next to his police cruiser. I pressed the fancy button that made the car window go down. "Daddy!" I yelled out the window. As soon as we stopped, I jumped out and raced to him. "The new car is awesome. You've gotta come smell it."

He scooped me up in his arms and gave me a bear hug. "I will in a little while." He put me down and then took my mom by the hand. They walked toward the office. I followed them in.

When we entered the waiting room, the nurse behind the desk sprang up. "Come right in."

My father turned to me. "You'll need to wait here, Simplicity. Mommy and I have to talk with the doctors."

"Okay." I turned and scanned the room filled with kids and pregnant moms. Seeing some cool toys in the corner, I went to sit and play.

As I waited, I watched the ladies rub their big bellies. Their stomachs looked like they were about to explode. I squirmed. How does the stork get the baby to come out? I looked down at my stomach and pressed on my belly button wondering if it had something to do with that.

After a few minutes, I noticed some of the nurses behind the glass talking as they looked out at me. I smiled at them, but that made them sad. One came out to ask how old I was and if I wanted a snack or something. I told her I was six and that I wanted to save room for ice cream because we were going to celebrate. Her face went white. She nodded slowly and then walked off.

It seemed like forever went by as a new group of moms came and went. Finally, my dad and mom returned. The way they both looked, I didn't think we were going for ice cream.

My dad went over to the nurse behind the glass window. "Is it all right if I leave my police cruiser in the parking lot overnight? I'd like to drive my wife home."

I thought the nurse was about to cry. "Yes, of course, that's fine."

"Thank you." He looked to me. "Are you ready, Simplicity?"

"Yeah." I jumped up and followed.

The ride home was quiet. My dad never let go of my mom's hand. I stared out the window feeling sad. I wasn't interested in the new car with all of its buttons anymore. For some reason, now, it didn't seem important.

When we pulled into the driveway, I started to climb out of the car. "Hold on a minute, Simplicity," my dad said. He kept his eyes fixed on my mom. I watched him, watch her.

My mom shook her head. "Robert." She started to cry. He leaned over and held her in his arms. I squeezed the door handle, unsure what to do. After a moment, she glanced at me; her eyes filled with tears. She squeezed them shut and curled herself into my dad's shoulder. "I can't tell her." Her voice cracked. "I can't..."

"It's okay, Maggie." He stoked her hair.

She swallowed. "I think I need a few minutes by myself."

He nodded. As she stepped out of the car, he held her hand until his arm was outstretched. After my mom walked in the house, I looked to my dad.

He pinched in between his eyes. "Why don't we stay out here and give your mom a few minutes."

My voice shook, "Okay."

"I need to talk to you, Simplicity." He patted the front seat. "Come and sit up front?"

My eyes widened. "Upfront? Can I?"

"Yes. Just this once."

I slid between the front seats and sat down. I'd never been allowed to sit up front before.

My dad bent his head forward and gripped the steering wheel. I'd never seen him so upset. I felt bad, but I didn't know how to help. "Daddy?"

He nodded.

"Did the doctor tell Mommy that something happened to my baby sister?"

He looked up at the car's ceiling. "No, Pumpkin. The doctors said she wasn't pregnant after all."

I tilted my head. "I don't understand."

"She's got a lump growing in her belly."

"A lump?"

"Yes."

I was concerned and confused. "What kind of lump?"

"A bad kind."

I shook my head. "What does that mean?"

He took in a sharp breath before he spoke. "It means she's very sick."

"How sick?"

"The doctors don't know for certain yet, but they think she has the same thing that Grammy had."

I'd never known my Grandmother. She'd passed away before I was born. All I knew was that she died suddenly, and my mom and my aunts, who were still in high school, were left all alone.

"Daddy?" My body started to shake.

"Yes, Simplicity?"

"Do you mean Mommy might die?"

His face twisted in pain. Slowly he nodded.

My hands went cold. "My mom...." I shook my head trying to block out what I was hearing. "But she can't leave," my voice trembled.

"She's not leaving—she's not leaving." He shook his head repeatedly as he stared straight ahead.

I didn't want to believe it. My mom who kissed my scraped up knee when I fell off my bike, my mom who baked me a triple-chocolate birthday cake, my mom who read me bedtime stories and tucked me in at night, my mom was my whole world—she had to be there—always.

My chin trembled. It felt like my heart was ripping in two. I started to cry.

My dad reached out and pulled me into his arms. He squeezed me so hard I couldn't breathe. I reached up and hugged him around the neck. His badge poked me in the chest, but I didn't care. I did not want to let go of my daddy.

I looked up at him, hoping this was just a mistake. "Maybe…maybe…the doctors are wrong."

His eyes swelled with tears. "I'm sorry, Simplicity."

I let go of him. "No. No." I started to get angry. I shook my head as I climbed out of the car.

"Simplicity," he called out.

I ran toward the house. He followed.

I raced to find my mom. She was kneeling at the end of her bed. "Mom." I wrapped my arms around her.

"Oh, sweetie." She cradled me in her lap. My dad knelt down beside us.

We sat and cried—clinging to each other.

CHAPTER THREE

Melanie's Secret

Eight months had passed since my mom had been diagnosed with cancer. Things had changed a lot for all of us. I quietly crept out of the garage with the ten-speed bike that my mom had bought me at a yard sale; trying to be super quiet so I wouldn't wake her. I had barely finished tucking her into bed when she dozed off. It was funny how we had flipped roles. These days I tucked her in more, than she did for me.

We'd spent that morning at the "drips office." That's what I called it—the place the doctors said my mom had to go for her medicine. She would sit in this big, gray, scary-looking chair for hours while they dripped some stuff into her arm. She laughed when I called it that one day, so the name stuck.

Once I reached the sidewalk, I hopped on my bike and began my daily patrol, imagining all the stuff a six-year-old girl could do if she ruled the world. I would cruise around my neighborhood, right up to the edge of where it was safe to ride, keeping a watch on everything.

When I took the corner toward the entrance to our subdivision, I saw the oddest sight—a chubby, little girl with oversized glasses dragging a large suitcase behind her.

"Hey." I rode my bike past her and then circled back around. "Whatcha doing?"

"None of your business," she said in a snotty voice.

"Well it is my business." I raised my chin, sounding confident and in charge like my dad. "I keep an eye on stuff around here."

She ignored me and continued pulling the suitcase down the street.

Curious, I asked, "Whatcha doing with that bag? Are you stealing it?"

She stood up. "No! It's mine."

"What're you doing, then? Going on vacation?"

She huffed, "If you must know, I'm running away."

I was shocked to hear that. When I was mad, I usually retreated to my tree house and moped. This girl looked to be around my age and the thought that she was tough enough to gather her bags and just take off impressed me.

"Why you doing that?"

"Because my parents don't love me." Her face looked sad.

"Why would you think that?"

"My sister told me." She yanked at the handle and the bag scraped along the asphalt. "And they never like anything I do."

"Never?"

"No. If I bring home an A-, they ask why didn't I get an A+. If I win second prize, they ask why didn't I win first. They hate everything I do." She looked like she was going to cry. I felt bad for her. When I messed up, my mom and dad would always give me a hug and tell me I'd do better the next time.

"Sounds to me like they're dumb."

She stopped and put both hands on her hips. "They're not dumb. They have PhDs."

I had no clue what that was. "If they think second place isn't awesome, then I think they're dumb."

"Sounds to me like you're the one who's dumb," she moped.

I squinted at her. "Are you defending them now?"

She looked away. "Maybe."

"Well, I might be dumb, but I'm pretty sure you're not gonna get very far dragging that suitcase down the street."

"I'm fine."

"Uh-huh." I made another loop around her with my bike. When I saw how close we were to the main road, I got worried. My dad had told me never to ride my bike near it. He warned me that there were bad people in this world who might try to hurt me.

She scowled. "Why don't you just leave me alone?"

"Because you look like you need some help."

She panted, "Well, I don't."

I tried to think of some way to change her mind. "You got any money?" I asked.

"No."

"You got any food?"

She stopped. "No."

I shook my head. "And I'm the dumb one."

She glared at me. "I'm leaving, and nothing you say can stop me."

"I'm not gonna stop you." I pushed out my chin and stood tall straddling my bike. "I'm gonna help you."

She looked at me—suspicious.

"Back at my house I've got some money saved from my allowance. If you come with me, I'll give it to you."

She bit her lip.

"You can get something to eat, too," I added.

She wavered a little.

I stopped in front of her. "And after that, when you have supplies and stuff, then you can run away."

She looked down at her heavy bag. "I guess," she said, still hesitating.

"What's your name?" I asked.

"Melanie."

"Hi, Melanie." I offered her my hand. "I'm Simplicity."

She shook my hand. "That's a pretty name."

I puffed out my chest. "Thanks."

We stood there for a moment, just getting used to each other. I noticed her shoulders were starting to slump. She looked tired. "Do you want me to help you carry that?" I said, pointing to her bag.

Her head lifted. "Oh, could you?"

"Sure. I think we could balance the bag on my bike seat and walk it back to the house together."

"That'd be great."

It took a few tries, but we finally got the bag to balance on top of the bike. It teetered like a seesaw between us as we walked home.

I pulled out Oreos, milk, and my change jar for her, but after we ate, she had forgotten her plans to run away.

"Here, check out this dress." I handed her my doll with silver evening dress.

When she reached out to take it from me, I noticed a big, purple bruise on her arm.

When she caught me looking at it, she quickly pushed down her sleeves.

I pointed at her arm. "How'd you get that?"

"What?" she said, startled.

I put my hands on my hips. "The big bruise, silly."

"Oh, that." She fussed with the trim on her sleeve. "I fell off a swing."

I squinted. Now I was the one who was suspicious. "You must have been swinging pretty high to get a bruise like that." She kept her head down and didn't answer. Just then, my mom peeked in on us. "Hi, Mom," I said. "We didn't wake you up, did we?"

"No, honey." She tilted her head as she looked at Melanie. "Who is this?"

"Melanie." I smiled and stood up tall, proud I had made a new friend. "She lives in our neighborhood."

"Nice to meet you, Melanie," my mom said. Melanie gave a shy nod. My mom smiled then went into the kitchen to make dinner. Melanie squeezed her hands together.

"Everything okay?" I asked, concerned about my new friend.

"I'm worried," she whispered. "Are you going to tell your mom what I was doing?" Her body shook. "I'm worried she'll tell my parents."

"No." I shook my head. "Never. It'll be our secret." I patted her on the shoulder trying to make her feel better.

She smiled. "I like you, Simplicity."

"I like you too, Melanie."

After that, we were always best friends.

CHAPTER FOUR

A Walk in the Woods

Maggie Kendall

Maggie Kendall sat in her soft, Queen Anne's style chair, quietly knitting. On top of the braided navy rug on the living room floor was her daughter Simplicity, playing with her dolls.

Maggie had spent the last eleven months imparting as much wisdom as she could to her young daughter, doing her best to prepare her for what lay ahead without her mother there to guide her.

Knowing she had very little time left, Maggie carefully considered what was the most important legacy she could pass on. She thought of all the many things a girl needed to know to survive in today's modern world. All the hard lessons she had learned over her thirty-six years about work, family and life. One rose to the top. She wanted her daughter to know that she was loved.

"Should I pack up and get ready for the drips office?" She asked without looking up from her game.

Maggie put her knitting needles down. "Why don't we skip that today and do something together, just us girls."

She raised her head and beamed. "That sounds awesome, Mom." Then Simplicity squinted and wrinkled her brow. "But is it okay? Isn't that place supposed to make you well again?"

Maggie swallowed, knowing what the doctors had told her. At this point, nothing will help.

"I think spending time with you is more important."

"Okay." Simplicity popped up onto her knees. "What do you want to do?"

Maggie looked around and then out their sliding glass door into the woods that bordered their backyard. "Why don't we go for a picnic? We can walk down to the creek."

"That sounds great."

They made up a lunch and packed it into a large, wooden basket. Holding the picnic basket between them, each one took a handle. They walked out the back door and up the path that ran behind their home. Maggie smiled at the lopsided slant of the basket.

They strolled along the trail that meandered beside Stone Bottom Creek. Maggie looked up into the lush, green canopy as she inhaled the sweet scent of the forest. A gentle breeze tickled her skin. It was a perfect summer day.

When they found some flat rocks, they sat by the creek and ate their sandwiches. "This was great, Mom. I love the wrap you made, and the brownie is terrific. Double chocolate chunks. My favorite." She bit down.

Maggie smiled. As the water trickled down over the smooth face of the rocks at the bottom of the creek, a squirrel raced by with a nut in its cheek. "Isn't it beautiful, Simplicity, all this wonderful nature all around us? Never forget that even the little animals are taken care of."

Simplicity, with a mouth full of brownie, looked up at her mom and nodded.

"No matter where you go, I believe God will be watching over you."

"Just like you and Dad?"

Maggie bit her lip, as her heart broke. "I may not always be there, but I want you to know how much I love you."

"I love you too, Mom."

After they ate, they packed up and headed back to the house.

"Well, what should we do next when we get back?" Maggie asked.

"Oh, there's lots of things I been wantin' to do. We can get out my paintbrushes and maybe make a card for daddy. Or we could bake some cookies. I saw a bag of chocolate chips in the pantry when I went to get the picnic basket."

Maggie smiled as Simplicity went on about all the fun things she had been wanting to do. She patiently listened, until she felt a strange warmth spread in her stomach. She looked down at her abdomen.

" . . . Dad said this fall he would take us on one of those boat trips where they go and watch the whales. Doesn't that sound like fun?"

Maggie stopped walking, suddenly feeling lightheaded.

"Mom?" Simplicity turned to her.

Maggie dropped her side of the basket.

Simplicity went to help her. "Are you okay?"

"I'm all right," Maggie said as she stumbled toward a large granite boulder. "I need to sit down for a moment, but I'll be fine."

"Here let me help you." Simplicity took her by the elbow.

Maggie stroked her daughter's little hand. "Thank you."

"Is everything alright?"

Maggie sat up straight, not wanting to frighten her. "I'm okay. I think I overdid it today, that's all."

Simplicity nodded, apprehensively.

Maggie grimaced as a sharp pain ran across her stomach.

Simplicity put her hand on Maggie's shoulder. "Mom?"

Maggie reached out and squeezed her daughter's arm. Her voice wavered. "I think I might need some help."

Simplicity took a step back, her eyes wide. "What should I do?"

"Run back to the house and call your father at the station." Maggie pressed her arm across her abdomen.

Simplicity nodded rapidly. "Okay. Are you sure you'll be okay here by yourself?"

"Yes." Maggie forced a smile.

Simplicity turned to leave, but Maggie reached out and caught her daughters hand. "Simplicity." She squeezed. "Never forget how much I love you."

"I love you too."

In a flash Simplicity turned and ran up the trail. Maggie watched her young daughter, giving it her all.

At the crest of the hill, Simplicity glanced back over her shoulder. Fighting back the pain, Maggie nodded. She dug her palm down into the hard rock, attempting to keep up the façade. After her daughter disappeared into the woods, Maggie's body gave way. She slumped onto the rock.

Her vision blurred. She whispered down the trail, "I love you, Simplicity."

Then, she let go.

CHAPTER FIVE

Robert's Secret

Robert Kendall
Eighteen Months Later

Backing out of the driveway, Robert Kendall paused before driving away from his home. This was the first night he had left his daughter's side since his wife had passed away a year and a half ago.

The pain of losing Maggie still pained his soul. The hole in his life where she had once been was an open wound that seemed like it would never heal. He missed his sweet wife so much. Everyday tasks, once done together had now became an agonizing torture of remembrance. Every night he'd fall asleep staring at her empty pillow, and every morning he'd wake up reaching out for her—leaving him feeling as empty as his arms. He couldn't let anyone pack up her belongings; it hurt too much. Her dresses still hung in the closet next to his uniforms. Robert was numb inside, hanging on for his daughter's sake, overwhelmed with the heavy weight of being alone.

After arriving at the Kiwanis Lodge, he drove around the small parking lot searching for a parking space. What few spots there were in the pothole-filled lot were occupied by police cruisers. He parked in the back corner next to the dumpster and headed in the front door.

The lodge was an old throwback, built during the boom period of the 1950s. A long, curved, wooden bar with brass railings hugged the left side of the structure. In the back corner, a doorway led to a kitchen. An open room with a wooden parquet floor dominated the rest of the building.

"Chief Kendall," Officer Clemmons yelled from the back of the room while lifting his beer mug high. The smile on the young officer's face warmed Robert's spirits. He had arrived late to the bachelor party on purpose, hoping to drop in and make a quick appearance before heading right back home. The groom-to-be was one of his young officers, Deputy Jonas Smythe. Even though he hated bachelor parties, he knew it would be viewed as an slight if he didn't show up, at least for a little while.

"Chief." Deputy Smythe's greeted him at the door. "Thanks for coming."

"I'm glad to be here."

The best man, Officer Jeremiah Thompson, hopped up from his seat, brushed back his curly brown hair and came over. "Can I get you a drink, sir?"

"A ginger ale would be fine. Thank you."

"Are you sure we can't get you anything stronger?" Smythe's arm swung wide as he gestured toward the long J-shaped bar. "Thanks to my generous best man here, it's an open bar tonight." He patted Jeremiah on the back.

Robert took a long, deep breath and glanced around the room. He hadn't planned to drink, but everyone was having such a good time. He didn't want to bring the festivities down with his sour disposition. "Yeah, I guess one's okay."

The young officers glanced at each other and exchanged a quick smile. The groom headed back to chat with his guests, while Jeremiah walked with Robert to the bar.

"Cyndi?" Jeremiah waved to the blonde bartender. "This here is Chief Kendall."

She smiled warmly. "Nice to meet you."

"Cyndi is my wife's cousin. She's the one that got me the deal on the room tonight."

"Hi, Cyndi. It's nice to meet you." Robert nodded politely.

His finely tuned investigative mind clicked into overdrive, filtering her, as he did with every new person he encountered, through a list of wanted posters and police sketch-artist drawings. He couldn't shut off the maddening habit. She was good-looking. He'd guess, in her mid-thirties, though she appeared younger because of the way she carried herself. Her blonde hair was clearly a dye job but suited her. She wore too much makeup in Robert's judgment, though he had to admit that it was a modest level of makeup for this type of job.

She smiled. "What can I get for you, Chief Kendall?"

Jeremiah leaned onto the brass railing and added, "She makes a heck of a Speeding Bullet."

Robert snickered. "That's a little bit too fast for my lane."

She laughed.

"I'll stick with a beer," he said.

"How about the house draft? It's got a little, extra kick." She flashed her blue eyes in his direction. "If you think you can handle the ride."

"Sure."

She turned and walked down the narrow bar past a mountain of liquor bottles.

Robert leaned his elbows on the brass railing and snagged a peanut from the nearest bowl. He glanced over at Jeremiah. "One of the ladies at the station heard a rumor that someone was planning to hire a stripper." He broke open the peanut shell. "But I reassured her none of my officers have that poor judgment." He flipped the nut into his mouth and eyed Jeremiah coolly.

The young officer coughed and straightened up, "No, sir. That was just a fleeting rumor you heard."

"Good." Robert took another peanut.

Cyndi came back with the beer in a frosted mug. "Here you go. A tall drink for a hometown hero." She winked. He wasn't sure if she was being flirty, or just friendly.

"Thanks." He nodded and then stepped away from the bar and went to join his men who were sitting around a collection of circular tables loosely pushed together.

"Chief." The group of officers straightened up as he approached. Even off duty, Robert knew how intimidating he was to his men. It didn't help that he was like a roaring lion around the squad room this past year and a half. The soft side his wife could coax out of him had shut down without her.

Determined to loosen up for the sake of morale at the station, he slapped Deputy Ross on the back, spun a chair around, and straddled it. "Steven, tell me how's your family?"

Deputy Ross smiled and launched into a long description of his kid's exploits. The proud father recounted every detail of how his nine-year-old son had caught the winning touchdown pass during a peewee football game. "Mindy was so ecstatic that she jumped up and spilled her soda all over the poor guy in front of us." Everyone laughed, except Robert. He was imagining what might have been if his wife had lived. Half-heartedly, he continued to listen, trying to appear happy and engaged. Inside, however, his heart ached. Even though Robert was in his forties, the weight of life's trials these last few years weighed him down. He felt like an old man whose life was nearing sunset.

The party continued. The officers hooted and hollered as they drank and had a good time. A few had organized a round of darts, and everyone was betting on who would win. Judging by the number of darts that missed the board—embedding themselves into the wall—Robert could tell his young officers were enjoying the free drinks.

As Robert took another sip of beer, somewhere from the back of the kitchen, a door slammed shut, followed by a frantic, female voice shrieking, "Get out of here!"

Robert jumped to his feet. Cyndi backed out of the kitchen and stumbled behind the bar. A split second later, a man Robert didn't recognize, charged through the kitchen door straight at her. The guy reached out and grabbed her by the arm. Robert rushed through the small opening between the bar and kitchen and came right up behind them. Robert scanned the man, checking for any bulges under his clothing. "What's going on here?"

"None of your business," the guy snapped.

Sizing him up, Robert estimated he was in his early thirties, a buff six foot one. Robert gestured for Officer Clemmons to get a pair of handcuffs. "Let go of the lady's arm and back away," Robert said in a firm voice.

"F— you."

Every chair leg in the place scraped on the hardwood floor as the crowd of police officers rose to their feet.

Robert wanted to diffuse the situation before it escalated into violence. He kept calm as he spoke. "Listen, why don't we talk outside."

"There's nothing to talk about." The guy glared down at Cyndi. "My tramp of a girlfriend thinks she can put a restraining order on me." Then the jerk swayed. Robert could smell the liquor emanating off the guy.

"Get out of here, Chad. You're supposed to stay away from me." Cyndi tried to pull his fingers off her arm.

Chad tightened his grip. Robert wanted to react, but he knew Chad needed to let go of Cyndi's arm before he acted. At the other end of the counter was Jeremiah. Robert gave him the heads up to be prepared to jump over the bar when Robert made his move.

Trained to handle volatile situations, his voice remained calm. "Son, this doesn't have to escalate into violence."

"Shut up, old man, or I'll kick your ass in."

Years of dealing with violent offenders had forged Robert's instincts. He knew it was time to act. The problem was the narrow corridor behind the bar kept the perp between Robert and Cyndi.

"Leave me alone," Cyndi yelled.

Robert could see she was trembling. He locked eyes with her and did his best to convey one thought: *Trust me.* As Cyndi's eyes fixed on his, her expression changed.

"You must be the stupidest person alive." She glanced back to Robert.

He nodded his head, encouraging her to keep going.

"When you pulled in here, didn't you see the parking lot filled with police cruisers?" Emboldened, she stood tall and defiant.

Robert smiled at her.

The young man raised his head.

Robert seized the opportunity to instill fear in the perp. "Cyndi is an in-law of one of my officers. All of whom are right now itching to show you the full meaning of— excessive force.

Chad looked around the room.

"Me standing here is the only thing restraining them."

Chad wavered and let go of Cyndi's arm. Robert reacted. His adrenaline surged and everything slowed. He drove Chad to the side, away from Cyndi. Chad reached out and tried to use her as a shield, but Robert, anticipating the cowardly move, acted faster. His right hand seized Chad's wrist as his bodyweight smashed Chad into the sea of liquor bottles. Robert snagged Chad by the shoulder and pivoted him around while yanking up on his right wrist. The tactical move swept Chad around like a rag doll. Then Robert slammed him onto the bar.

Jeremiah, who had hopped over the rails, grabbed Chad by the wrists as Clemmons tossed the handcuffs to Robert. Promptly, Robert snapped them on. Knocking over more bottles, Chad struggled to get loose. "This is police brutality and I have witnesses," he shouted.

"Shut up," Jeremiah snapped. A few of the other officers came to help pull Chad out from behind the bar. As they dragged him off, Robert looked around for Cyndi. Huddled underneath the bar, on the floor in the corner, she was curled up in a ball with her arms wrapped around her knees.

He walked over to her and squatted down. Gently, Robert reached out and touched her shoulder. "Are you all right?"

She nodded her head, but he could see she was shaking.

"We'll lock him up. He won't bother you again."

"Thank you," she said softly. With wide eyes, she gazed up at him.

Robert looked her over for injuries. Seeing none, he said, "Why don't we get someone to take you home?" He helped her up. Holding her steady by the elbow, he looked across the room and caught Jeremiah's attention. Jeremiah came over.

"You okay, Cyndi?" Jeremiah took her by the arm.

"Yeah, I'm fine," she said gruffly, "I can take care of myself." She pulled down the hem of her shirt and straightened up.

Chad screamed, "I want a lawyer."

Cyndi shook.

Chad rambled on, "I want to talk to a judge and tell him all about this bit—."

"Watch your mouth." Officer Clemmons cut Chad off before he could finish the insult.

"Chief?" Branson walked over to Robert. Robert stepped out from behind the bar. "What should we do with this guy?"

"Call up." He turned to Deputy Ross. "Who's on duty?"

"Grant and Johnson."

"Call up Grant and Johnson. Read the guy his rights, emphasizing his right to remain silent, then take him outside. Have them charge him with assault and battery as well as violation of a restraining order." He glanced over at Cyndi. "Then tell them to stick his carcass in the drunk tank until he dries up."

"Yes, sir." Branson and a large group of officers orchestrated Chad's hasty departure.

"Chief?" Jeremiah came over. He nodded toward Cyndi. "I'm worried he might have an old set of keys. I've got a call in to Billy Barnes to get her locks changed."

"Good."

Jeremiah lowered his shoulders and looked around the room. "The thing is none of us were planning on driving this soon . . . do you think you could—"

Robert put up a hand. "Say no more. After she gives her statement, I'll take her home."

Jeremiah nodded. "Thanks, Chief." He walked back over to Cyndi.

Robert watched her from across the room as she went right back to work cleaning up the mess. As Jeremiah spoke to her, she waved him off as if all of this was nothing, but when she reached out for a glass, Robert could see her hand trembling. He could tell—her tough exterior was just an act.

CHAPTER SIX

Into the Night

As they drove, Cyndi didn't say a word. She just stared out into the darkness. The transparency of her reflection in the window added to her vulnerability.

When they reached the apartment complex, Robert asked her to wait in the police cruiser while he conducted a thorough room-to-room search of her apartment. After he was sure it was clear, he came out for her.

"You should check to see that nothing is out of place."

"Okay . . ." She walked around her small apartment, nervous, checking every inch. The apartment was packed full of mail-order boxes, everything from Amazon to Zayre's—most unopened. "Everything seems to be fine."

"I'm glad. The locksmith should be here shortly."

She nodded.

"I'll get going then." He headed for the door.

"Oh." She stepped forward and reached her hand out. It hovered in the air for a second. "Would it be too much to ask you to wait, until he arrives?"

"Your ex-boyfriend is locked up. He won't be getting out any time tonight."

She glanced sideways. "He's not my ex-boyfriend. He's just some creep I helped out once, and then he started following me around."

Robert's brow furrowed. "How does he have a key to your apartment?"

She squeezed her arm and looked downward. "...I lent him my car one day. That's how I helped him out. I was worried he might've made a copy of my keys."

"Oh." Robert rubbed at his neck.

Her blues eyes widened.

"I can stay until Barnes gets here."

Cyndi's face relaxed with relief. "Oh, thank you so much."

"No problem. I just need to call home."
He went to pull out his cellphone.

"Oh, please, use mine." She gestured toward the kitchen phone.

When Robert dialed, she walked into the living room.

His warmhearted neighbor, who offered to babysit, answered the phone, "Kendall residence."

"Good evening, Mrs. Granville. Thank you for watching Simplicity tonight. I was wondering if it might be possible for you to stay later than we planned."

"Of course," she said. "I'm so glad to hear you're having fun."

"Regrettably, work pulled me away."

"Oh . . ." Mrs. Granville sounded deflated. She had retired years ago. With little excitement in her life, busy boding was now her vocation.

"I might be late."

"Is everything okay?" she asked.

He noticed Cyndi peeking at him. He turned away. "Yes, fine."

"It's no problem at all. We're having a wonderful time."

"The guest bed is all made up if you'd prefer to sleep over. Simplicity can show you where we keep everything."

"Oh. That's sounds like fun—a girl's slumber party—I haven't had one of those in years."

He smiled. "Thank you again. May I talk with her?"

"Sure." She called out, "Simplicity, your dad's on the line."

He heard his daughter bounce to the phone. "Hi, Dad. Are you having fun?"

"Yes pumpkin, but I won't be home until late."

"Okay. I'll make you breakfast in the morning, and then you can tell me all about the party."

He smiled. His daughter delighted in making him breakfast on the weekends, just like her mother had. "That sounds good. Don't forget to say your prayers."

"I won't."

"I love you."

"Love you too, Dad."

Robert hung up the phone and stepped out of the kitchen.

Cyndi smiled. "Your daughter?"

Facades Crumble

"Yes."

"She has a beautiful name."

"Thanks."

She looked past him into the kitchen. "Can I get you something to eat?"

His phone vibrated. "No, I'm fine." He pulled the phone out and looked down to see a text message from Jeremiah. Reading it quickly, he grimaced.

"Everything okay?"

"Yes, but unfortunately the locksmith had an emergency call. A driver locked himself out of his car in the middle of the highway. Billy's going to be a while I guess."

"Oh . . . if you want to go that's fine, really."

"No, it's okay. I was more worried about my daughter." He glanced at the kitchen phone. "But she seems fine."

Cyndi nodded, and then looked at him with a curious expression. "Can I ask you something?"

"Sure."

"Why would someone get out of their car in the middle of the highway?"

Robert chuckled. "From the sound of it, I think nature called."

"Oh." She giggled.

He smiled, enjoying the sound of her laughter. After she fell silent, they stood there for an awkward moment. She hurried over to the living room and removed a box from the couch. "Please, sit down. Can I get you a cup of coffee, Chief Kendall?"

"Call me Robert." He ran his fingers through his thick hair, and then sat down on the loveseat-sized sofa. "And no, thank you, I'd be up all night if I drank coffee now."

"Let me see if I can find something else for you." She walked into the kitchen.

He glanced around the apartment. Besides the clutter of packages, it was very clean. The boxes, though, he found a bit curious.

She opened a cabinet. "How old is your daughter?"

"Eight."

"That's a sweet age."

"Yes, she's my sweet Simplicity."

Cyndi pulled down a couple of glasses. "That's an unusual name. What made you choose it?"

"My wife, Maggie. She had a hard life after her mother died. She raised her younger sisters by herself. She liked the old days back when she was a kid. When things were uncomplicated—simple. She wanted our daughter to never forget that carefree time, when the wholesome pleasures in life are pure and unpolluted." He stared in silence.

"That's nice. She sounds like a wonderful woman."

He swallowed, but said nothing.

Cyndi returned carrying two drinks. She handed him one and sat down.

Robert took a sip. He stopped, looked down at the glass and cleared his throat.

Cyndi saw his expression. "Oh, it's Jack and Coke. I thought you'd prefer a nightcap."

"Thank you." He nodded politely, but put the drink down.

They sat and talked for a while about innocuous things: the weather; how Jeremiah and her cousin met; how Cyndi had moved from California nine months ago.

Running out of subject matter, she glanced around the room. "I read in the newspaper about that project your department is advocating. It sounds like a good thing, helping kids who don't have anyone looking out for them."

"The skate park?" Robert grinned. It had come to be a source of comfort to him these last few months. "I wish everyone felt that way. They'll be voting on it soon, and I'm concerned it's not going to pass."

"That's too bad. I think a lot of people have no clue what it's like to live on the wrong side of the tracks. No one watches out for you." She pulled her legs up underneath herself. "I'd like to help. Is there anything I can do?"

He smiled. "Thanks. That's a kind offer but there's nothing left to do right now, except vote."

She nodded. "Does your daughter skateboard?"

He chuckled. "No, Simplicity prefers her bicycle."

Thinking about his eight-year-old daughter, he realized how much his whole life had revolved around her the last year and a half. He'd forgotten what it was like to have a casual conversation with another adult. He leaned over and picked up the drink.

"Do you live here alone?" Immediately, he regretted the mixed signal that question might send. Quickly, he added, "I mean, do you have a roommate?"

"No. I thought about it once, but I'd feel uncomfortable having someone else live here...unless we were good friends." She looked around the room. "Since moving here I've been so busy working. I haven't had time to make friends with anyone."

He reached out and took another sip of his drink. As he did, his wedding ring clinked on the side of the glass. He noticed she stared at the gold band for a moment and then turned forward, dropping her feet to the floor.

He looked down at the ring and felt awkward. He twisted it around his finger a few times. Seeing her changed body language, he worried about appearances, "I think I need to explain."

"You don't need to explain anything. You've been a perfect gentleman."

"But I don't want to give you the wrong impression." He squeezed the ring—hard. "My wife passed away a year and a half ago."

"Oh." She turned back. "I am so sorry."

She put her hand on her chest. He made a slight nod.

"I can't imagine what that must feel like, to lose someone so close."

He clenched his jaw.

"It must have been very hard on your daughter."

"It was—is." He took another sip. "She and her mother were very attached."

Cyndi pursed her lips as she kept her gaze lowered. "It must have been hard on you, too."

He glanced up and their eyes briefly lingered.

"How long were you married?"

He took in a deep breath before speaking. "Sixteen years."

"Wow! That's wonderful. I read in a magazine that the average marriage lasts seven years. It's good to hear there are still strong relationships out there."

Robert realized how blessed a man he had been—even if those days were over.

She stared at the wall.

He did as well.

Distracted in thought, she absent-mindedly spoke. "I have no idea what it feels like to be that loved."

Robert felt deep sympathy for her. "You've never married?" He took another sip.

"No." She smiled nervously, embarrassed. She looked at the empty wall. "Nobody's ever asked me."

He studied her for a moment. "Beautiful, nice girl like you, that's hard to believe."

She smiled.

His head began to feel the effects of the alcohol. "You make a good drink, too." He held up the glass.

"Thanks."

As he turned it in his hands, the light from a lamp reflected in the glass. "I guess I've turned into a lightweight in my old age."

She softly chuckled. "You're not a lightweight, and you're definitely not old."

Robert's gaze traveled back to her face. "You must have dozens of young guys knocking at your door."

She blushed and shook her head.

He watched her beautiful blue eyes modestly looked toward the floor. Then, she smiled back.

Robert began to let himself imagine what it would feel like to be close to someone again. As the empty hole in his heart widened, part of the numbness began to crack.

"Robert . . ." Cyndi swallowed.

He looked into her eyes that seemed to grow softer. "Yes?"

She tucked her hands underneath her legs. Faintly she said, "Are you as lonely as I am?"

The tenderness in her words released a sorrow in him. Feeling her ache, his pain was never more acute. He looked at this vulnerable, young woman and wanted to reach out and hold her.

She gazed up at him with a softness in her eyes that she hid behind her tough facade.

Robert put down his drink. "We're two broken people, aren't we?"

As their eyes remained locked, she leaned forward. Tenderly she kissed him, and then pulled back.

The smell of her hair, the soft touch of her skin and the ache in her eyes, drew him in. He reached out. She slid onto her knees, leaned over him, and wrapped her arms around his neck. The feeling of a warm body pressed up against his filled up his lonely void. As his hard shell crumbled to the ground, he kissed her. He took her into his arms and drew her down onto his lap. They kissed passionately. Her supple lips and tender touch stirred feelings in him, long since buried. One thing rapidly led to another as loneliness and alcohol all played their part into the night.

CHAPTER SEVEN

Consequences

The next morning when Robert awoke, his head was pounding. He looked down at the unfamiliar maroon-colored comforter and realized he hadn't slept in his own bed. The events of the night before splintered into his mind. He closed his eyes and cursed himself, "Damn it."

The aroma of fresh brewed coffee roused him from his sulking. Groping around for his clothes, he dressed and headed to the kitchen. Cyndi was at the stove making breakfast. Dressed in a long T-shirt, she reached for something in the upper cabinet. When he realized she had nothing on underneath, he turned away. Guilt washed over him.

She spun around and smiled. "Good morning, sleepyhead. I hope you're ready for breakfast." She bounced over and gave him a peck on the cheek. She turned to return to the kitchen, but he gently caught her by the arm. He lowered his head and spoke softly, "I need to apologize."

She looked at him, puzzled. "For what?"

"For what happened last night."

"Is that all?" She swatted the air and returned to cooking. "It was fun."

He ran his fingers through his hair. "I don't want you to take this the wrong way, but what happened." He looked toward the bedroom. "It was wrong."

She cracked an egg. "What do you mean?"

He exhaled.

She shook her head. "Why would you even think that?"

"I want you to know how sorry I am for taking advantage of you."

She laughed. "Taking advantage of me?"

"Yes. You were emotionally vulnerable last night. I shouldn't have stayed."

She grinned, mischievously. "As I recall, it was me who asked you to stay, then I plied you with alcohol and kissed you."

"Yes, but given what happened to you last night with that jerk stalking you—"

"Who? My ex?"

He raised his head. "What do you mean? Your ex?"

"My old boyfriend."

Robert's body went rigid. "I thought you said he was just some creep who'd been following you."

"Sort of, partly . . . but, we did date."

Robert's face drained of color. "You dated him. For how long?"

"A few months."

His mouth fell open. "Why did you lie to me and say you hadn't?"

She shrugged her shoulders and her dyed blonde hair rolled down them. "I was worried. You seem like a straight-lace type of guy, and I didn't want you to think I was a slut."

Robert froze.

She looked at him perplexed. "What's the difference?"

"There's a big difference. I'm a police officer. I'm sworn to protect and serve. I just arrested your boyfriend and then took you to bed." He squeezed his forehead. "I can't believe I did that . . ."

"We had sex. It's no big deal."

He looked at her in shock. "It is to me."

"Yeah." She smiled and looked off. "Last night, I thought you were digging it, so I kept going with the knight in shining armor thing."

He put his hands up and stepped back. He realized the shy, sweet girl he had imagined last night was nothing more than a mirage.

Oblivious to his distress, she asked, "Do you want salt on your eggs?"

"No. I have to get home. My daughter needs me."

"Okay . . . I guess."

"Thank you for the offer of breakfast." He started to leave.

She followed him with the frying pan in her hand. "Hey, you're not one of those 'Wham, bam, thank you ma'am' type of guys, are you?"

He stared straight through her. This girl was not what she appeared to be. "Cyndi, right now I need to go home and figure some things out."

"You'll call me, right?"

"Yes, Cyndi. I will."

He grabbed his jacket, stepped out the door and zipped quickly down the stairs.

When he reached the car, his reflection in the window stopped him cold. He glared, appalled at himself for his wanton behavior. Then he looked up to the sky.

Forgive me.

CHAPTER EIGHT

What Will Be Will Be

Robert sat at his desk studying the transcripts from his testimony in a domestic violence case, when he noticed across the squad room Officer Jeremiah Thompson, in plain clothes, anxiously pacing the hallway. Jeremiah was off duty today. Robert wondered why he was there. When Jeremiah noticed Robert looking at him, he let out a breath, stepped forward and headed straight toward Robert's office.

Robert waved. "Come in."

"Chief," he said, anxious. "Can I talk to you for a moment?"

"Have a seat." Robert gestured toward a chair.

Jeremiah sat quickly, and then began to bounce his knee.

Robert slid his paperwork to the side. Jeremiah was cool under pressure; his obvious distress was out-of character. "What's this about?"

Jeremiah exhaled. "Chief. I need to speak to you off the record—man to man."

Robert had been expecting a conversation like this for weeks. He was glad to get it over with since he still felt guilty about what had happened that night between Cyndi and himself.

"Okay. Let's talk. Off the record."

Jeremiah spoke firmly. "I know that good men can get tempted. I don't need to hear an explanation of what happened that night between you and Cyndi. You're both adults." He cleared his throat. "But my wife is very upset by all this."

Robert nodded.

"She and I want to know what your attentions have been toward Cyndi, since then."

Robert didn't like the accusatory tone. He tried to put aside that he was Jeremiah's superior and not take offense. "Jeremiah, your wife's cousin and I shared a special evening together."

Jeremiah shifted in his seat.

"I wanted to see her again. Cyndi, however, never returned any of my phone calls. I assumed I had misread her intentions toward me. So I let the matter drop."

Jeremiah furrowed his brow. "She never called *you* back?"

Robert nodded.

Jeremiah straightened. "So you wanted to pursue a relationship?"

"Yes. Yes I did."

"And you haven't spoken to her?"

Robert looked down as he fussed with a pen. "Not since the morning after."

Jeremiah exhaled.

Robert waited.

Jeremiah slid the chair underneath him closer to the desk. "Chief...Robert." He softened his tone. "I'm sorry to have to tell you this."

"What?"

Jeremiah closed his eyes. "She's pregnant."

Robert jaw clenched.

"She told my wife a few days ago."

Robert sat, rigid. "Is she certain, she's pregnant?"

"Yes. She's been to the doctors already."

Robert rubbed his forehead, hesitant to ask his next question. Jeremiah must have guessed what he was thinking. "Yes. It's yours."

Robert felt like the floor had dropped out from underneath him. "Jeremiah. Regardless if Cyndi wants to have a relationship with me, I want to reassure you that I will be doing the right thing, by her and the child."

Jeremiah grimaced.

Robert stiffened.

"I'm sorry." Jeremiah shook his head. "I know Cyndi has a problem with lying, but I never thought she would..." His voice faded.

Robert knew there was something else he held back. "Jeremiah. Just tell me what it is."

"She told my wife that you wanted nothing to do with her, or the baby."

Robert shook his head. "That's not true."

"I knew that didn't sound like you, especially after what you and your wife went through to try to have a second child."

Robert's chest tightened.

"I could tell something wasn't right with her story. That's why I came to the station to talk to you." He paused before continuing. "She called my wife this morning and told her she couldn't afford to raise a child by herself."

Robert ran his finger along the edge of the desk.

Jeremiah took in a deep breath before continuing. "She was calling from her car on the way to the abortion clinic in Freemont."

Robert felt like a freight train had struck him. "How long ago did she call?"

Jeremiah looked up at the clock. "About an hour ago."

Robert rose to his feet and headed for the door.

Jeremiah jumped up. "Chief. Chief." He tried to catch up. "What are you planning on doing?"

"I'm not sure." He ran his hand through his hair. "But I have to do something."

Jeremiah put on his coat. "Let me drive you."

"No. I can't ask you to go." Robert pulled out his keys as he headed for the parking lot.

Jeremiah raced up next to him. "Maybe I can try and talk to her. Anyways, I'm not sure you should be driving."

Robert looked down at his hands. "Fine." He handed Jeremiah the keys.

The men jumped in the cruiser and took off.

"I don't know how much time we have." Jeremiah gestured toward the on button of the flashing lights. "Do I have permission?"

"No," Robert leaned forward, "but I do." He flipped the switch and the lights and siren went full blast. They raced up the highway to Freemont County.

After they arrived, Jeremiah went to call his wife, while Robert parked the cruiser down the street. As Robert sat in the car by himself, he berated himself for the multitude of mistakes he made that night. How he wished he could go back in time and rewrite the past.

Jeremiah walked back to the cruiser and stepped in. "She said the appointment was at ten o'clock."

Robert nodded.

"Delicate situation." Jeremiah looked at him, uneasy. "How are you going to handle this?"

"I have no idea."

"My wife told me some stories about when they were kids—Cyndi can be difficult." Robert ran his thumb along the edge of the steering wheel.

Jeremiah continued, "They say that a liar's punishment isn't that no one believes them, it's that they can't believe anyone else."

Robert nodded.

"You're an honest man, Robert. But she may have trouble believing you."

As they sat and waited, a host of things flooded Robert's mind. He felt helpless. He knew if Cyndi wanted to go through with this, there was nothing he could do. He hadn't known Cyndi long enough to even guess what she was thinking. From what she had gone through in her life, she was probably scarred and hurt.

Robert looked out the windshield at the road. Now here she was—alone and pregnant—because of him. She probably thought he was just like everyone else from her past. As a cop, he was supposed to be different—protect and serve. Instead, he had added to her troubles.

Jeremiah pointed. "Here she comes."

Robert sat up.

"Do you want me to go and talk to her?"

"No. I need to do this." Robert took off his holster and slid the gun toward Jeremiah. "Thanks for all your help."

"You're welcome. Good luck."

Robert stepped out and walked up the sidewalk towards Cyndi. She stopped suddenly when she saw him. "Cyndi. I'm sorry to startle you. I'm not here to frighten you, or stop you, if this is what you want to do."

She stood frozen in place.

"But I'd like to tell you some things first." He tilted his head. "May I?"

Her expression softened for a moment, but then her tough exterior refortified. "Nothing you say is going to change my mind."

Robert inhaled. "The day after we were…together. I was unsure of the stories you'd been telling me. Some events didn't make sense. I was concerned. So I went and did a background check on you." Her head snapped up. "I know you have several outstanding arrest warrants in California."

"It's just for some bad checks I wrote." She stepped back.

He gestured trying to reassure her. "I'm not here to arrest you. What I wanted to tell you was that I read the court transcripts of what your lawyer said had happened to you when you were younger."

"Isn't that supposed to be private?"

"No. Not when you're in an open public court, pleading for leniency from the judge."

She glanced down.

"I know you've had a hard life."

Her face flushed.

"And I know you lied to me about a lot of things."

She squeezed her arm. "I have a problem with buying things." The image of those boxes in her apartment flashed into Robert's mind. He nodded. She continued to look down. Robert studied her expression.

"Even though you lied to me, I'm pretty sure you were being honest about one thing you said that night."

She looked up to him, curious. "What was that?"

"That you've never felt what it was like to be loved."

Her hard face, softened.

"So despite the things you've done in your past, I called you the next day to ask you out for dinner."

She looked down and bit her lip. "I thought you were just calling to bang me again."

He closed his eyes. "No. That's not the type of man I am."

She looked at him, warily. Robert could see the swelling of emotions barely contained behind her eyes. "I'm not going to try and stop you if this is what you choose to do." He gestured toward the brick building. "But I wanted you to know, I like you. And I see something good in you."

Her eyes started to well up.

"The time we shared together meant something to me. And I would really like to pursue a relationship with you, if you'll have me."

Her mouth fell open. "If I'll have you?" She pointed at him. "You're too f—ing good to be real."

He lowered his eyes. "I'm not good."

She looked at him in disbelief. "Yeah, right." She wiped at her nose with the back of her hand. "They all dump you eventually for someone younger, anyways." He grimaced, knowing what had happened to her.

Slowly he said the words, "Cyndi…not all men hurt."

Her lower lip trembled.

Robert held out a hand.

Cyndi looked up to him with hope in her eyes. Then she nodded, but didn't move.

Robert walked to her, wrapped his arms around her, and held her close.

She burst into tears.

CHAPTER NINE

Run

Robert Kendall
Present Day

"Robert, look out!" Detective Frisco yelled right before the bullet struck.

Robert raised his weapon and shot at the oncoming gunman. The three rounds hit their mark. Two in the chest. One in the arm. The last shot sent the gun ricocheting into the mud. The perp fell to the ground with a thud.

Gun leveled, Robert scanned the area. "Clear." He raced around the cruiser to his fallen colleague. Detective Frisco lay on his face slumped in the grass.

"Code 3. Officer Down," Robert shouted into his shoulder radio. He knelt down. "Ken." Robert checked Ken's body attempting to locate the entry wound. A small torn piece of shirt revealed the location. Frantically, Robert searched for signs of blood to try to stop the bleeding.

Ken moaned. "Uh…"

In the darkness, Robert couldn't see the wound. "Where are you shot?"

"Shot?" The Detective groggily responded. "In…in…in the vest."

Ken rolled to the side. Robert leaned closer and pulled back the officers shirt. The bullet had lodged against the back of the vest and flattened into a silver mashed pancake.

Robert exhaled. "Are you okay?"

"I hit my head when I went down. What the hell happened?"

"I don't know. They got the jump on us. Someone must have tipped them off."

Ken looked toward the gunmen who lay in the mud. Robert's eyes followed. The man gurgled. Robert exhaled, stood up, and then went to help the man that had just tried to kill him.

CHAPTER TEN

Lockers

Simplicity Kendall

I tried to sneak by, but Tabby must have seen me. She called out over the crowd of kids, "Simplicity? Where are you going?"

I stopped short. "Nowhere." Sheepishly I turned to face her.

Tabitha slipped her arm around mine and walked beside me. "You sure have been acting strange these last few days."

Defensively, I countered, "Why do you say that?"

"Come on. Whenever anyone is talking to you, your eyes are always darting around the room, checking out who's coming and going. What are you looking for?"

"Nothing."

"Yeah right."

I lowered my head, trying not to make eye contact with "Gabby Tabby." She was the last person I wanted to confide in. Especially about the fact that I'd been trying to sneak off from the rest of the group to keep an eye out for Jake. Over the last few days, Jake had quickly developed a reputation as the school's resident bad boy. I'd barely seen him since that first day, except from a distance. Whenever my eyes locked onto the back of his head he seemed to sense it. One second he would be walking smoothly through a crowd of kids, and the next he'd vanish. It was infuriating trying to pin him down. He was a drifting riddle, a murky, dark cloud with no clear edge. So, I nicknamed this brooding shadow of a young man the "Black Enigma."

When Tabby and I reached my locker, I began pulling out books for my morning classes.

"Simplicity?" My head snapped up when I heard my name called. I turned to see Gabe, all bright and cheery with his dirty-blond hair tousled to the side. He strode toward me in between the row of lockers.

"Hi, Gabe." I turned back to fuss with my schoolbooks.

"I've been looking for you." Gabe casually leaned up against a locker, while Tabby silently retreated. "How are things going?"

I looked up into his deep, gleaming blue eyes; I found myself smiling back without meaning to. "Good."

He scanned my face. "How's your chin?"

"Fine."

"I'm glad to hear that."

Over Gabe's shoulder, I noticed a bunch of heads tilting in our direction, eavesdropping. Gabe, Jake, and I had been the hot topic of gossip these last few days. Anyone with fresh gossip would be the center of attention in class. If they played their cards right, they could dangle the fresh news out to the other students like steak to a tiger. I shook my head. I hate small schools.

Gabe pursed his lips. "I was wondering if you'd seen Jake around?"

My head whipped up. "No. Why do you ask?"

He pulled the black T-shirt Jake had lent him out of his backpack. "I'm just trying to give this back to him."

"Oh." I pointed toward my own backpack propped in between my legs. "I planned to do the same today."

"I haven't seen him once since the first day of school. Sort of strange in a school our size." He casually glanced around. "Do you think you could give this back to him?" Gabe held out the shirt.

Thinking this would strengthen my hand to spark a conversation with the floating Black Enigma—if ever I cornered him—I jumped at the opportunity. "Yeah sure."

"Cool." As I took the shirt from Gabe, our hands briefly touched and a static spark snapped between us.

"That was weird." He smiled at me as he shook out his hand.

"Yeah." I rubbed my fingertips.

The bell rang out the two-minute warning that homeroom was about to start.

Gabe looked back over his shoulder at our audience and then stepped closer to me. I kept my gaze downward trying not to look into his eyes. He was like a male siren, luring my ship onto the rocks.

He began slowly. "I was wondering—"

"Gabe. Where've you been?" Matt zipped around the corner, followed closely by the rest of Gabe's usual pack. "We gotta go. We'll be late for class."

Gabe moaned, and then turned around and looked directly into my eyes. A curious chill ran through my body.

"Are you gonna be around during lunch?" he asked.

"Yeah, why?"

He kept his eyes on me while stepping backward. "I got something I wanted to talk to you about." He flashed me one of his melt-'em-like-butter smiles, the kind he nonchalantly gave out to the girls to make them swoon. But as I watched his expression, something looked different about it. It didn't look fake.

"So, will I see you at lunch?" he asked again.

Gabe was always Mr. Suave, but the way he was acting right now, I swore he was a little self-conscious. "Yeah. I'll talk to you then."

"Great." He paused and waved a finger. "Oh, and tell Jake I have something for him in my car."

"I will."

He smiled briefly, then smoothly turned around to his friends and cruised off.

Tabby reappeared. She slid up behind me and gave me a soft elbow to the ribs. Practically purring, she said, "Oh . . . now I know what you've been looking for."

"What?" I asked, trying to diffuse my embarrassment.

"Don't what me, girl." She eyed me up and down. "I know you all too well. I could tell something was different."

I tried to hide my blush. "Nothing's different."

She nodded. "Uh-huh."

CHAPTER ELEVEN

Darn Those Floating Black Enigmas

The past few days I'd been covertly asking the ladies who worked in the main office about Jake. It turned out to be an exercise in futility. They knew less about him than I did. The more I couldn't solve any of the riddles surrounding him, the more my curiosity grew. I had a bazillion different questions I wanted answered: Where did he live before? Why did he have to leave suddenly? How come he dressed the way he did? Why was he sweet and kind one minute and then scary-fierce the next? Whose gun and ammo was that? And most importantly, who was he protecting?

During physics class, I volunteered to bring the morning attendance paperwork to Mrs. Prescott, the Assistant Principal's secretary. She was a silver-haired woman who used to work for my dad at the police station until her husband got sick. She needed to work steadier hours during the day. She adored my father because he'd pulled some strings and got her transferred to the high school without losing any of her benefits.

Casually, I began milking her for information. "So what's this about?" she asked as she filed the papers I'd handed her along with those from the other classes.

"I'm doing a write-up for the school newspaper on the three new kids who started here this year. I was trying to help them fit in and stuff." This was true enough. I was writing a short blurb for the school paper, and I did want to help them fit in—one especially.

"Oh, that's sweet."

I smiled and nodded. The note-taking app on my smartphone sucked, so I flipped open a little paper notepad. "So, do you have any information about . . ." I looked down and feigned ignorance of his name, "Jake Hanson?"

She tilted her head to the side and scrunched up her face. "No, dear," she answered absently, but then she stopped filing, turned, and raised a finger. "Except I did overhear Dottie in the cafeteria say his father started working in Derrybrook with her husband."

"Oh." I nodded.

"Dottie mentioned the father seemed very nice."

"Huh?" I mumbled. That didn't quite jive with what I knew of Jake's father, but, then again, many people could be clever about appearing upright in public while their private lives could be quite a different thing. I kept peppering her with questions about Jake and the other kids without giving anything away. Unfortunately, she knew next to nothing.

"I'm sorry I can't be of any more help. Maybe you should go and interview them directly."

That's exactly what I've been trying to do.

"I've spoken to the two girls but this . . . Jake. He's been hard to find."

"Oh." She went over to another filing cabinet. "Here we are." She pulled out his folder.

Man, I would love to get my hands on his paperwork.

"He has second period study in the library with Ms. Hatchett."

Gold!

"Great. Thank you for all your help." I smiled sweetly, grateful for her assistance.

"No problem, dear, and don't forget to tell your father that my husband and I would love to have you all over for dinner. Anytime he wants."

"Thank you. I'll tell him." I headed back to my science class, anxiously counting down the minutes until second period.

After class ended, I finagled a pass from my study hall teacher and went to stake out the library. Hiding behind a shelf of books, I watched the doorway, waiting to pounce. No way was I letting him escape me this time.

Just as the second period bell rang, and Ms. Hatchett, the school's librarian, began to close the door, he slipped in.

She gave him one of her famous prune faces. "Young man, I do not tolerate tardiness," she said in her distinct acerbic tone.

"Sorry—" He turned around. When he looked at her, his face lit up, as if he had met an old friend, but just as suddenly, he grimaced, turned, and began to rush away. "Sorry ma'am. Won't happen again," he said over his shoulder as he scurried off.

I tapped my fingers on the shelf as I watched him head straight for the only hidden part of the library—the research room. He opened the door and disappeared inside.

I debated my next course of action. Should I give him the shirts and hurry away, or do I stay and try to unravel this mystery? My heart pounded when I remembered our encounter in the closet. His arms clamped around me. His eyes ablaze. I swallowed.

With trepidation, I approached and peeked in through the glass. Alone, he faced the reference books that lined the back wall. He sat in one of the six maroon, aging, vinyl chairs that circled the small oak conference table. He seemed lonely. I let out a heavy sigh, turned the doorknob, and walked in.

I wanted to sound confident, but my voice betrayed me and cracked out a geeky, "Hi." Before he even saw who it was, his head rose as his body stiffened. I walked around the small conference table and pulled out the chair directly across from him. His hands pressed onto the table as his ripped forearms tensed. He leaned forward. "What are you doing?"

Underneath the table, I squeezed my hands and fought back the urge to bolt. Then I said the first thing that popped into my head: "Sitting."

He made a face like he'd swallowed a bug. "Why are you sitting in here?"

For some unexplained reason, his annoyance fed my failing courage. I quipped back, "There aren't any chairs in the hallway."

"I don't want you anywhere near me."

I ignored the insulting remark and kept going. "It's a free country. Besides, the study room's for all students to use, not just you."

He swallowed, and his Adam's apple rose and fell.

"Anyway, I have something for you." I pulled out the shirts from my backpack and slid them across the table.

He eyed me suspiciously, grabbed the shirts, and dumped them onto the chair.

Then he flipped open one of his schoolbooks and focused his stare downward at the page. "Well, you've made your delivery." He gestured toward the door. "You can get out now."

I sat for another minute, watching him, but he didn't make eye contact. Instead, he kept his head down as he glared holes in his book. Here was a guy who was doing everything he could to tell me to get lost, but for some inexplicable reason it was having the opposite effect. Something different about him just kept pulling me in.

"Is that what you want—for me to leave?"

"Duh," he cracked. "Have I been too subtle?"

Determined, I rummaged in my backpack and snagged the first book I felt. "I would leave, but I need to use the reference books in here."

Jake looked down at the textbook I had pulled out and raised an eyebrow. "You need reference books to study geometry?"

"Yeah. I wanted to research . . ." I glanced around the room trying to come up with some excuse, however dumb. ". . . where the Pythagorean theorem started."

He snickered. "I'll give you a hint. It started with Pythagoras."

"Is that so?" I flipped open my notebook and pulled out a pen. "Then I'm off to a good start."

He stifled a chuckle.

Taking that as a good sign, I forged ahead. "Anyway, if you don't like being in here with me, why don't you leave?"

He glanced out the window. "Because I'm stuck in here avoiding Lemonade-Face McCabe."

I laughed. "Mel used to call her that."

Then a shiver ran up my spine. Melanie called her that at the beginning of our freshman year before Mrs. McCabe got divorced. Then she changed it back to her maiden name—Ms. Hatchett. She stopped using McCabe years ago. How did he know her old name?

I shifted in my seat.

"Who's Mel?" he asked.

"A friend."

"Mel?" He furrowed his brow. "Is that a boyfriend?" His expression tensed.

"No. It's my girlfriend. It's short for Melanie."

His face relaxed. "Oh." Then he returned to glaring at his book.

I continued to prod. "So why are you hiding?"

His face curdled. "I'm not hiding. Why would you say that?"

Now it was my turn to pour on the sarcasm. "You said you were avoiding her. Avoiding's the same as hiding—tomato, to-mah-to."

He didn't respond.

After a second, I leaned the palm of my hand against my cheek and began flipping pages in my textbook. We sat for several minutes in this weird showdown. Occasionally, I would look up at him, but he never looked back. Debating, I glanced down at my backpack wondering if I should even give it to him.

I inhaled and rallied my courage. "I have something else for you."

"Uh-huh," he mumbled.

I pulled the phone out of my bag and placed it on the table in between us.

He looked at it, puzzled. "What's that?"

"A phone."

"I know it's a phone," he said sarcastically. "Why are you giving it to me?"

"Because you lost yours when you saved me from falling."

He raised his head. "How did you know that?"

"I saw you put down a phone on top of the wall before the fight. I guessed that was your phone I saw plummet past my head and into to the ground."

He stared at me.

"Am I right?" I watched him closely, trying to judge his reaction.

Slowly, he nodded.

"I couldn't afford a brand new one. This one's refurbished." I slid it toward him. "It came loaded with sixty minutes of air time. After that you have to buy more."

He hesitated at first, but then he reached out and examined the smartphone.

"I saw your head buried in your phone that morning, and I felt bad that it got destroyed on my account." I returned to flipping pages in my math book.

He started strumming his fingers on the thick, oak table. "Listen, Simplicity, I appreciate this." He held up the phone. "And for you covering for me, but, I can't accept it." He put the phone down and slid it back over.

"Why not?"

"Because I don't think I should have anything to do with you."

"That wasn't how you were acting the other day," I said pointedly.

"I changed my mind."

"I don't believe you. I don't think you've changed your mind."

"Well, you're wrong."

"I don't think I am."

He cocked an eyebrow. "Are you ever wrong?"

I looked up at the ceiling. "On occasion."

"Well, this is one of those times."

I don't know why I decided to open up first and say the words aloud—but I did. "I want to get to know you, Jake."

He scanned the bookshelves behind me. "No. You don't. You have no idea what I'm like. If you did, you'd run."

"Do I really have to say how much of a cliché that is."

"In my case it's not."

Skeptically, I asked, "Are you really that evil?"

He closed his eyes for a tense moment. When he opened them, he pierced me with a steely, cold gaze. "Yes. Yes, I am."

The hair on the back of my neck flew straight up. It felt like the temperature in the room had dropped to match the ice in his eyes. Everything in me screamed, *run*, but I didn't listen. "Sorry. I don't think you're bad at all. I think this is just an act you have to drive people away."

"It's no act."

"Well, then you need to take acting lessons, because you suck at scaring people off."

The corner of his mouth shook, like a dam holding back too much pressure. His lip twitched, and then he broke into an uncontrolled laugh. He shook his head. "Why can't I frighten you away?"

I kept me gaze down as I casually turned another page fighting back a grin of victory.

"I like you, Simplicity. I do." A crooked smile uncurled across his sour face. "You've got spunk."

I looked up and his gaze met mine. "Thanks."

His eyes softened for a brief second, then he shook his head and spoke sharply again. "But I don't want us to be friends."

His words were meant to hurt and they did. I tried to hide my disappointment but failed. He looked at my sad expression and exhaled. "It's just . . . I probably won't be here very long."

The thought of him moving on so quickly panicked me a bit, though I had no clue why. All I knew was that I was getting nowhere, smacking up against this concrete wall time after time. I decided to reverse tactics. If he wanted to be cool and aloof— so could I. Coldly, I stated, "I never said I wanted to be your friend. I said, I want to know more about you."

His expression immediately changed; I couldn't tell if he was hurt or angry. Either way, I felt badly that I was forced to resort to saying it, but I kept going. "I want some answers." I leaned back and crossed my arms. "If you expect me to help you keep up this charade."

"Is that all?"

"Yes."

He sat there for a moment, thinking. Out of the corner of my eye, I caught Ms. Hatchett prowling in between the rows of books. I snapped my head forward and pretended to read. "Put your head down," I whispered.

Like a prison guard making her rounds, she came walking by the window and looked in on us. We kept up the façade, pretending to be deeply engrossed in our studies until we were sure she had moved on.

Jake broke the tension. "Fine. I don't know how many answers I'm gonna give you, but you can ask—if that'll placate you."

"Great," I mockingly responded, hoping to hide the fact that I was elated he wanted to talk. "All right." I straightened up and cleared my throat, stalling while I mentally categorized my list of questions from most to least important. This was my chance and I didn't want to blow it.

I glanced around the research room— very aptly named at that moment—and decided to go for broke. "Whose gun and ammo was that in your living room?"

He swallowed. "Technically, my dad's."

"Does he know it's illegal in this state?"

He bit the inside of his lip as he stared at me. His eyes searched my face for a moment before they tempered. "Yes. Yes, he does."

"Where did he get it?"

He paused before giving me an answer. "The evicted tenant who lived there before us left it behind."

"Why would they do that?" I queried.

"Crack addict." He raised an eyebrow, "Enough said?"

I gave a sharp nod. "Why is your dad keeping it, then?"

"For protection."

"From what?"

"Burglars."

I scoffed at his pat answer.

He looked offended. "The house has been broken into a few times already."

I recalled that odd, broken glass on the front of the mobile home. "Is that why the duct tape is on the window?"

Yeah, he looked at me a bit impressed. "Yeah. You noticed that?"

I nodded.

His chin lifted, revealing an expression that was a mix of alarm and wonder. "You're pretty smart."

"Not really." I kept my eyes focused on him. "Just observant."

He cocked an eyebrow. "I'll keep that in mind."

"That would be the wise thing to do."

He grinned. "So what else do you want to know, Sherlock?"

My mouth opened and closed as a flush rose to my cheeks. I loved the compliment, which then caused me to forget my next question. I chuckled and shook my head. "If one didn't know any better, one might think you were actually starting to enjoy opening up."

Looking directly into my eyes, he smiled. "I'm enjoying something else, actually."

His chocolate brown eyes widening, coupled with the subtle meaning behind his words, caused my stomach to spin. Immediately, I dropped my gaze. Interrogations don't work well if one loses their head to the subject.

Elated I had gotten him talking; I refocused and went to my next question. The whole Hatchett-McCabe issue popped to mind. "Where did you go to high school before?"

"Home."

"Home?"

He stuck out his chin defensively. "Homeschooled."

"Oh . . . that explains it."

"Explains *what*?" he snapped the last word.

I couldn't help myself—I chuckled. He was on a teeter-totter, going back and forth between defense and offense with every question I asked. One moment his eyes would soften, and I'd get just the smallest glimpse of something warm behind his icy exterior, but in the next, the door would slam shut. I looked at him, trying hard not to show how much he was growing on me. His scowl continued to increase as he waited for my answer.

"Homeschooled." I said. "Explains why you're so smart."

The unexpected answer caught him off-guard. Losing his tightly held self-control, he began to laugh.

"Shh . . ." I placed my index finger over my mouth. "Her ears are like a hawk's."

He searched up and down my face. "So you're not one of those anti-homeschoolers then?"

I shook my head and recollected the still tender memory of my mother lying propped up on pillows on the couch, textbook in hand. "No. My mom homeschooled me for a year."

"Yeah."

Talking about my mom, I felt the tension roll off my shoulders. "She homeschooled me so we could spend more time together after they gave her the news."

Jake's smile turned into a confused frown. "What news?"

I whispered the vile word I loathed: "Cancer."

"I'm sorry, Simplicity." He swallowed. "Is she better now?"

I clenched my jaw. As he watched me intensely, he squeezed both fists.

"She passed away when I was seven."

The last of the ice melted from his eyes. "I'm really sorry."

I nodded, trying to push down the growing tidal wave of grief threatening to drown me. "She died less than a year later." I stared at the closed door.

"That must have been really hard."

"She was so strong, right up until the end."

"Your mom sounds like a special lady."

"She was—is." I bit down on my tongue, still not able to admit after all these years that she was really gone.

"She must have been a great mom."

I squeezed my fist. I'd buried my emotions for so long. I'd never really opened up to anyone about how much her death hurt me. Not even with my dad. Remembering her and how sweet she was, I felt overwhelmed.

His voice was soft. "You miss her, don't you?"

I nodded. "It's been ten years . . . but the pain of losing her is still so raw."

I looked at Jake. Like a mirror, I could see the same deep pain that seared my heart, reflected in his eyes. The dark, brooding young man was gone and an innocent, fresh-faced boy gazed back at me. He'd felt deep suffering too. I could feel a shared brokenness connecting us. He reached across the table and brushed back a stray piece of my hair.

I felt a lump in my throat as I stared into his eyes. I bit my lip—brown eyes always reminded me of my mom's. As the flood of emotions rose within me, I started to weep. Jake cradled my cheek in his hand and stroked away a tear with his thumb. We sat there gazing at each other, immersed for a moment.

"Simplicity." He swallowed. "I want to tell you something. It's about..." His eyes darted around the room as if he was debating, then he pressed his lips together and leaned forward. "It's about my mom—"

CHAPTER TWELVE

No!!!

The study room door swung wide open and clipped the back of a chair. The jolt shattered the calm. I jumped in my seat and Jake jerked back.

"Is your name Jake Hanson?" Ms. Hatchett marched through the door with her face buried in a clipboard.

He scrunched down and kept his face turned away from her. "Yes."

"Since you're new here, you've never had my freshman orientation lecture," she said in her tart annoying tone. "There are numerous procedures you need to follow when you're in my library."

Internally, I groaned. Ms. Hatchett was a stickler for rules, and she loved to reign supreme over her little corner of the world—the high school library.

Jake's shoulders dropped. "I really don't need any instructions, ma'am."

"Oh, I beg to differ." She walked straight at him.

His eyes flashed franticly from right to left like a caged animal. My suspicions that he knew her from somewhere flared up once more. I jumped up and interceded. "Ms. Hatchett?" I said in my most angelic voice. "Mr. Wanes, my English Literature teacher, suggested I should come and speak to you."

"He did?" Her face looked like a question mark. "What for?"

I lowered my voice and spoke softly. "He's having me write a paper for submission to the National Writer's Digest. The subject this year is Teachers of Distinction."

Her eyes lit up.

I slipped my hand gently under her elbow and began to led her out the door. "Mr. Wanes thought, and I agreed, you would make an excellent story." This was partly true. After he gave me the assignment, we started discussing a few teachers I might want to interview. I had jokingly suggested that Ms. Hatchett was a teacher of distinction because of her distinct sour disposition. He laughed in agreement, but then quickly backpedaled. Clearly he did not want to lower a fellow teacher in front of a student—no matter how accurate the description.

I led Ms. Hatchett away from the research room.

Her head raised. "Well, that sounds interesting, my dear."

I could tell she was on the hook. "All I'll need is a short interview. I'll ask you some basic questions, like what inspired you to become a teacher, who are your favorite authors." Then I thought of a new question. "Where did you teach before coming here."

"My schedule is very busy . . . but, I suppose I could make time."

"Wonderful." I led her back to her desk. "Well, I'll be in touch." I smiled and started to zip off.

"Oh, Simplicity," she called after me.

Darn. Not fast enough. I turned interlinking my hands behind my back. "Yes ma'am."

She raised a finger while flipping through her clipboard. Knowing what she was about to say, I looked over at the clock and spoke before she could say it. "Boy. Look at the time. Class is just about to end." I hoped she hadn't memorized all the new class periods yet. She glanced at the clock and her face soured.

Worked.

"Tell that young man," she ran her finger down the list, "Jake . . . that I'll expect him to present himself to me the next time he enters the library."

"Yes, ma'am."

I didn't waste any time. I whipped around and headed straight back to the research room.

After stepping in, I leaned up against the door as I held the knob with my hands behind my back. "I think you have a problem."

He sat up straight. "What is it?"

"Next time you show your face in here, she plans to give you her famous library lecture."

"Great," he said sarcastically. Then he started packing up his books. "Is she coming now?"

"No. I faked her out and got you a reprieve."

He looked back over his shoulder at me. He smiled and that cute dimple popped out again. "Thanks."

"You're welcome."

He returned to packing his bag. I wondered what was rolling through his mind; was he planning to try to bolt anyway? I didn't want him to leave just yet, and I didn't know when I would get another chance like this. I walked over to him. "I do think you should wait until the bell rings and the other kids start heading toward the door—blend in with the crowd. If you want to get by her unnoticed."

He stopped what he was doing and nodded his head in agreement. I sat back down, hoping we could return to our conversation. I felt like he and I were finally starting to connect.

He glanced over his shoulder out the window. Trying to ease his distress, I suggested, "Perhaps you can have one of the office ladies switch your study hall to another classroom."

He nodded.

"If you need any library books you could just have someone else come in and get them for you."

"Yeah." He puffed out. "I'll get my large group of BFFs right on that." He flashed another glance out the window and then rubbed the back of his neck. I wondered what it must feel like to have to be constantly checking over your shoulder, worried all the time you're about to be found out.

"So . . ." he turned back around to look at me.

"So . . ." I glanced around the room.

"Aren't you gonna ask me any more questions?"

"Yes." I nodded my head. "There's one I want to ask, but, I'm sort of hesitant to hear the answer."

He looked at me perplexed. "You? Hesitant? This must be a doozy. What's the question?"

I looked at him, concerned. "Did you mean what you said?"

He wrinkled his brow. "About what?"

"About wanting to have nothing to do with me?"

His expression softened. "That wasn't exactly what I meant."

"That's what you implied."

He leaned back and sat there, looking at me for a long minute. I wished I could crack open his head and examine what he was thinking. Every time I thought I had peeled back part of the onion, another layer appeared.

He looked up at the ceiling and put his hands behind his head. "Honestly, I don't think you should have anything to do with me."

"Why?"

"Just 'cause."

I was worried my connecting flight was falling fast. Quickly, I tried to lighten the heavy load. Jesting I said, "You don't think I should have anything to do with you because at your last school you were a heartbreaker and treated all the girls like rotating flavors of the month?"

He made a big smile and rubbed the back of his head. "Hardly. I've been homeschooled since seventh grade. Only two members in my class—my brother and I."

"Oh, so you're really the leader of a he-man-woman-haters club, then?"

He chuckled. "No." He started to relax and stretch out his legs. "My family and I lived off the grid. We only came down for supplies every few months. I rarely ever saw a girl, let alone got near one."

I dropped my head and tried to hide my blush. He probably had no clue what he just inadvertently revealed. "So..." I spoke to the table. "You never got, close, to any girls?"

"Nope," he answered casually.

I gulped. I knew exactly what that meant. He was like me. "But you liked it up there?"

"Yep."

"So why'd you have to move?"

"Next question."

I snapped my head up. "Why is that innocuous query such a security breach?"

He laughed. "Innocuous query?" He shook his head. "Swallow an SAT prep book, lately?"

I wanted to try to keep the mood light, so I sang the words, "*You're avoiding . . .*"

He shifted in his seat. "With everything's a potential security breach."

I smiled affectionately, probing his defenses. He smiled back but still regally waved his hand, as he said, "Move along."

"Fine," I huffed. "Let's make a deal. I'll move off that subject if you agree to do something else."

He half-heartedly grumbled, "What?"

I tilted my head and said softly, "Accept my humble restitution." My gaze traveled to the phone.

He looked at me and then down at the phone. Picking it up, he pressed the screen. "Thank you for this. It's nicer than the one I had, actually."

"You're welcome."

He smiled broadly and his dimple appeared. I studied his face. When he was relaxed, his strong jawline seemed less menacing and more alluring. He shut off the phone and put it in his pocket.

I glanced up at the clock and realized I had only a couple of minutes left before class ended. There were so many things I wanted to ask, but he was clearly gun-shy, so leveling a bazooka at him right now would get me nowhere.

"What's your brother's name?"

"Connor."

"Does he like living here in Stony Creek?" I lowered my gaze and rubbed at my arm, trying to appear casual as I asked the question, "Or did he prefer where you lived before?"

He raised an eyebrow clearly catching my attempt at subtlety. "He's okay with it here."

"How about your mom, does she like living here?"

He snapped to attention, "My mom?"

"Yeah," I stared at him. "You started to tell me about her."

"She . . ." His voice faded. I watched him as he swallowed, deeply. His gaze drifted. I could see that pain floating in his eyes again. Lost in thought, his face soured, and his lips formed into a dismal grim line. I waited a moment for him to answer, but instead his head jerked suddenly like some unseen hand had slapped his face. His eyes narrowed and turned cold as that old, arctic stare returned. He leaned in and lowered his brow.

"Why are you doing this, Simplicity?"

I retracted back, startled by his sudden shift in mood. "I just want to get to know you, that's all."

He scanned my face. There was a frantic desperation in his eyes as his gaze hunted for an answer.

"No, you don't." His eyelids briefly shut and then opened as he came to some conclusion regarding my motives. "You don't give a damn about me or my family." He stood up and his chair flipped back slamming into the wall. "I'm nothing more than a riddle you want solved." He headed toward the door.

As a bolt of panic ripped through me, I wanted to yell, *no*. I didn't want him to leave, especially this way. I raced to block the door, which forced him to stop short. "Jake, that's not true."

His tall imposing frame stood towering over me. "Get out of my way, Simplicity. Get out of my way before I hurt you." His expression tried to intimidate me, but his voice cracked, betraying him.

I looked at the hard fierce shell that encased him, but my intuition felt sure there was someone soft hiding in the recesses. "I don't think you will," I said boldly.

He clenched his teeth and his face turned red. "You don't know what I'm capable of."

I swallowed. "I think you're all bark and no bite."

There appeared to be a million different riddles whirling around in his eyes. His jaw tightened, and his body hardened as he searched my face. Then he took me by the upper arms and looked straight at me. "I'm only going to say this once more. Leave me alone."

He was shaking so badly that his grip caused my arms to shake.

The bell rang, interrupting the tense moment. I stepped to the side, and he bolted out the door. I put my forehead against the wall and pressed my hand to it, trying to get my body to stop trembling. I shook my head. Why did I just do that? I stood silently, still shocked at the strange turn of events.

After I let his warning sink in, I realized something I should've done the first time I met Jake Hanson—have nothing to do with him.

Just let the wounded animal be . . .

CHAPTER THIRTEEN

Lunch

Later that day, red trays in hand, Tabby, Mel, and I shuffled down the lunch line with all the other little ducklings waiting to be fed by our surrogate mother birds, a.k.a. the cafeteria lunch ladies. The one bright spot so far in my miserable day was that that they were serving my favorite lunch, veggie pizza. Tabby stuck to her usual: an apple and skim milk. I looked down at her pitifully, empty tray and shook my head. "No wonder you're so skinny. You never eat anything."

Tabby laughed. "Are you kidding me? I eat like a horse!"

I countered using her patented catchphrase, "Uh-huh."

Unable to wait for the privacy of our table, she asked the question that had practically been dripping off her tongue all morning, "So what do you think Gabe wants to talk to you about?"

"Gabe, shoot." With everything that had happened that morning, I'd forgotten all about him. "I don't know." I shrugged my shoulders. "Maybe his mom and dad want to get together with my family, or something."

Melanie looked over at Tabby. "Is that all she thinks Gabe's interested in?"

Tabby, pretending like I wasn't there, looked past me and spoke to Melanie, "And here I thought she was the smartest one of our group."

"Gabe and I have been friends since we were kids—that's all." I sounded confident, but their ribbing got me thinking. Gabe did act a little unusual. My mind wandered.

A moment later, Tabby elbowed me. We had reached the end of the lunch line and Mrs. Stoddard held her hand out waiting to be paid.

"I'm sorry. What did you say my total was?"

She smiled. "$3.69"

"Thanks." I juggled my tray, then Tabby, Melanie, and I walked over to our usual table where Justine and Ally were already sitting.

"Hello, ladies. Guess who got picked for the Science Club?" Justine gave a short nod toward Ally.

"Congrats, girl." I high-fived her.

Tabby smiled. "That's awesome."

Ally's face lowered, she was always very modest, but I could tell she was enjoying the attention.

"Thank you," she said. Her voice was barely a whisper.

Melanie leaned in. "Tell me more."

She and Ally began their own private conversation. The cheerleaders, a table away, turned around and directed a few nasty looks my way via their artificial colored contacts.

"What's up with them?" I said, giving the heads-up to Justine and Tabby. They glanced over their shoulders at the cheerleaders, who then turned away.

Tabby raised an eyebrow. "Got me." She snagged one of Justine's fries and dipped it into the pleated white cup full of ketchup.

Justine leaned toward Tabby. "Has she coughed up any more information about what happened between her and Gabe on Tuesday morning?"

"No." Tabby pouted.

"So we have no idea what he's so hot-to-trot about?"

"Hot-to-trot?" I shook my head at them. "That's awful."

Ignoring me, Tabby raised a shoulder and turned toward Justine. "I think she's in total denial. She refuses to acknowledge why she has been acting so strange the last few days. I think I might have to stage another dating intervention."

"Oh, please, no."

"What?" She eyed me slyly.

"Tabitha Stanford Driscoll." I always broke out her full name when I wanted to make an impact. "I know you're just trying to egg me on. And it won't work." I pointed my fry at her.

She made an innocent face as she placed her fingertips lightly on her chest. "Who me?"

"Yes, you." I gave her a look and then bit down sideways on my fry. It crunched noisily as I chewed.

"Well, I guess we're about to find out what's going on," Justine nodded behind me. "Here comes Gabe."

I nearly choked in my hurry to swallow. I turned to see Gabe looking absolutely fabulous as he strolled across the cafeteria toward us. Conversations at nearby tables stopped as everyone turned to watch. I shook my head. Man, I hate this. It was high drama—American high school style.

"Ladies." He nodded.

The girls sang his name in unison, "Gabe." I could've puked at how easily my squad fell all over themselves when a good-looking hunk flashed them a smile.

He lowered his head in my direction. "I was wondering if we could talk, Simplicity?"

"Yeah, sure." I gestured toward the empty seat next to me.

He looked over at the girls and hesitated.

"Oh, you can talk in front of us," Tabby said with a grin. "Sit." She and Justine immediately turned toward each other and huddled, pretending to ignore us. Gabe looked at them and then straddled the bench.

"How's your dad doing?" he asked, still keeping an eye on my friends out of the corner of his eye.

"Good."

"My mom was asking about him yesterday. She'd been reading that interview with him in the paper about the big drug bust they made."

"Yeah. He's doing okay. I guess it was pretty rough that night. From what I overheard him saying to Cyndi." My dad never told me anything he did at work. I figured it was because he didn't want me to worry, but when it makes the local news, it's hard to ignore.

"Was it a meth lab or something?"

"I think so." I ripped off a tab of my napkin and rolled it into a ball. I knew from the tone of my dad's voice that night that something serious had gone down, but it wasn't until I saw the paper the next day that I realized the extent of what had happened. I didn't want to think about how close he came to dying that night.

"Drug addicts are scumbags," Gabe said harshly as he looked at the group of kids known as "the druggies" that sat in the corner of the cafeteria. I knew they occasionally smoked a joint now and then, just like the jocks, but for some reason they were stuck with the black sheep label.

I felt bad for some of them. I knew they had rough family lives. When you're left home alone most of the time, it's easy to get into trouble. Some of the ladies from the auxiliary club wanted to build a skate park to give them something constructive to do. The ladies sought help from my dad. He became an advocate for the project years ago, not long after Mom died. People gave him a hard time for it. He said it wasn't right that so many of those kids, mostly boys, had no father figure at home and that regardless of how they came to be in that situation, it was the mark of a good community to step in and keep an eye on them. He took some heat for it until he pointed out how much wiser it was to intervene early before the kids started to drift out of reach.

Gabe smiled. "My dad mentioned that he hadn't seen your father at the basketball league in a while."

"Yeah, Cyndi," I said caustically. I knew Gabe understood exactly what that meant.

"Sorry." He bounced his knee up and down. "How's your chin?"

"Good." I smiled. "Thanks for asking again. How are you feeling?"

"Fine." He bounced his knee some more. "Your dad never noticed?"

"I lucked out. He came home late from work that night."

"Oh good." He tilted his head. "I may have mentioned this before, but I want you to know that your dad scares me."

I chuckled. "The starting quarterback, who loves to charge down the field, is scared of something?"

He lowered his eyes. "Yeah, I get scared sometimes."

"I can sort of see it with my dad—since he carries a gun and all—but I can't imagine what else would scare you."

He leaned in so only I could hear. "I'm scared right now."

"About what?"

"What you're gonna say."

"What I'm going to say? About what?"

"About what I wanted to ask you."

I pulled back. "What did you want to ask me?"

"I wanted to know if you'd like to go out to dinner with me, maybe, tomorrow night?"

Oh, crud.

I froze. I so preferred the unemotional Vulcan-like logic of my brain to the tumultuous feelings of my body, but my stupid mind had completely shut down again, refusing to help me out of my predicament.

His deep blue eyes searched my face for an answer.

"Umm . . . I—" Tabby kicked my shin under the table. "Ouch!" I bent over to rub my leg as I scowled at her.

She and Justine mouthed the word, "Yes!"

I turned back to Gabe.

"Me? I thought football players gravitated more to the bobble-head cheerleader variety." I nodded toward the next table.

"That statement seems rather prejudicial to me. Like all guys who happen to play sports are the same?"

"Yeah, you're right. I'm sorry." I shook my head. "I'm elated, but, confused." My brow crinkled. "Why would you want to go out with me?"

"Are you kidding me?" He gave a short chuckle as he scanned my face.

When I remained silent, still waiting for his answer, he tilted his head. "You really don't know why, do you?"

Slowly I shook my head and shrugged.

Gabe looked around at the hoard of onlookers that now leaned in our direction, then whispered in my ear, "Go out with me, and I'll tell you why I think you're special."

I blushed range of crimson. The intimacy of the moment brought me up short. I just couldn't help myself as I let out a snort. He didn't laugh; instead, he lowered his brow and smiled as he tilted his head. He was disarmingly charming.

I took in a deep breath. I liked Gabe a lot and had known him for years but never considered he and I would ever get together, but then again . . .

"Okay. I will."

The look of concern on his face transformed into a broad smile. "Awesome."

My heart fluttered.

He scanned the sea of kids and stood up tall, giving the spectators their fill now that he knew my answer. "Six o'clock? I'll pick you up at your house?"

"Okay." I pressed my lips together and tried not to blush.

Gabe smiled, and then looked out across the room. "Finally. He appears."

"Who?" I asked, unable to see anything from where I sat.

"Jake."

I twisted around. There he was, watching us from across the cafeteria. I swallowed, unsure of what to make of his sudden appearance in the land of the living.

"Oh shoot. I forgot to tell him you had something for him."

"No problem." Gabe smiled at me. "I'll tell him myself."

I nodded, uneasily. I don't know why, but the idea of them talking to each other now made me nervous.

"I'll see you later," Gabe said.

"Yeah, see ya," I managed to say.

As Gabe walked toward Jake, Jake grabbed his books and began to walk off. "Hey, Jake," Gabe called out. Jake stopped.

I turned my attention back to my lunch tray and stared at the food my stomach no longer wanted to eat. I laughed when I looked up to see Tabby and Justine gawking at me with faces that emulsified two words: shock and awe.

"Stop it, you two."

"I think a train just hit her," Tabby said to Justine.

"It feels like it." I shook my head. "I didn't see that coming."

They both smiled at me. Looking past them, to the table beyond, I caught another round of evil glares from the cheerleaders nearby. I smiled back.

Then, out of the corner of my eye, I caught Gabe talking up a storm with Jake. Nervous, I swallowed hard.

The sharp sound of a tray smashing to the ground echoed from the back of the cafeteria. Everyone turned to look toward the bang. Seeing as it was nothing, I turned back. As I did, I looked in Jake's direction. He was staring over Gabe's shoulder— straight at me.

Tabby and Justine leaned in. "So, what did Gabe whisper to you?"

"I . . . I—" I couldn't stop rubbernecking at Jake.

"Tell us before we explode," Justine said.

"Gabe said he wanted to tell me how special I am," I said, still distracted by Jake.

Their mouths dropped open. "That's so romantic." Justine dreamily looked straight ahead as she ate another fry.

The next time I turned to look in the boys direction, Gabe gestured toward me and smiled. I smiled back. Jake glared at me with an expression that was part fury, part pain. For a second our eyes briefly locked, then he rushed away and disappeared once again into a sea of kids.

Damn . . .

CHAPTER FOURTEEN

My Two BFF's

On the bus ride home that afternoon, as my head rested on the window, I sat and stared out at the woods.

"Hey, wake up, sleepy head." Melanie shook my arm. "You're going to miss our stop."

"I wasn't asleep." I sat up. "I was just thinking about that day we first met. Do you remember?"

She smiled. "Yeah, how could I forget? You were so nice to me. You never did tell anyone that I had tried to run away, did you?"

"No," I said softly. I nodded to the seat behind us. "Not even Tabby."

Melanie smiled.

As the bus came to a stop, I stood up. A motorcycle with a loud muffler cut around the bus and roared quickly by. Our elderly bus driver, José, yelled and shook his fist as the black-helmeted rider sped past the entrance to my subdivision.

Tabby, Mel, and I stepped off the bus and walked past the old, faded sign that read: New Stone Bottom Creek Subdivision. Underneath the sign grew yellow petunias that some of the ladies from the Garden Club had planted at the base. The sign had faded so much now that the word "New" seemed sort of stupid. It had been twenty years since they built the subdivision. The developer went under, leaving some things unfinished—like a permanent sign. Just the same, I liked it here. It was a quiet neighborhood that backed up to the forest running along the edge of Stone Bottom Creek.

"What a day." Melanie exhaled as she heaved her loaded book bag over her shoulder. "I have so much homework. I'm going to be up all night."

"Why do you take so many classes?" I shook my head. "Two languages plus all those advanced studies."

She slid her glasses up. "I was talking to my sister last night. She said they're changing the requirements for college entrances to make it even harder. She said I would need to double up my classes if I wanted to be as successful as her."

"Prissy," Tabby sneered.

That's what we called Melanie's overbearing sister. Her real name was Charlotte I think, but we called her Prissy because it fit her personality so well.

Tabby went on. "Ever since the day I first came over to your house, she's been beating you down. She's at college now—doesn't she have anything better to do than to keep badgering you?"

"I know but—"

"Mels." I stopped and turned toward her. "You're smart. You're gifted. And with your high grades you're going to have your pick of any top college."

Melanie's eyes lit up. "Are you sure?" She was desperate for any positive reinforcement.

"Yes." I nodded. "I wouldn't say it unless I meant it."

She smiled.

"She is so right, Mels." Tabby took Melanie's book bag from her and carried it. "Don't listen to all that negative crap. It'll only bring you down."

"All right." Melanie nodded.

Tabby shifted the backpack over her shoulder. "Seriously, though—what on earth do you have in here? It's heavier than my bag."

"Well, that says a lot, doesn't it?" I chuckled.

"It's not that heavy." Melanie went to take the bag back from her. "It only feels heavy because you're all skin and bones."

Tabby swatted her away. "Are you kidding me; I'm as fat as a heifer!"

Melanie looked her up and down. "If you think you're fat, then I want to be a cow."

"Tabby, you're, like, pencil-thin," I added.

"Yeah, you so don't eat enough," Melanie said.

Tabby's face turned red with anger. "Let's drop the subject."

Melanie and I glanced at each other. Something was up, but now wasn't the time to start prying. I shot a look at Melanie. She pushed up her glasses and switched subjects.

"My mom told me about that drug bust your dad made."

Ugh . . . I so didn't want to talk about that anymore.

Tabby's face was grave as she spoke. "Those guys he arrested sounded scary. Did you see their pictures?"

I corrected her. "You mean mug shots."

Tabby nodded and went on, "Doesn't he get worried he's going to get shot or something?"

Melanie backhanded Tabby on the arm.

"Oh, sorry." She rubbed her muscle.

"It's okay," I said.

"I wasn't thinking," she said apologetically.

"He's fine. He always wears a bulletproof vest and everything."

I struggled not to think about how much danger my dad put himself in on a daily basis. He was never the type to sit back behind a desk and let somebody else place his or her life on the line. That's why he liked running the small police force here in Stony Creek. Since he was in charge, he could work alongside the other officers, helping whenever they needed it.

"He knows how to handle himself," I added, trying to reassure myself. I saw the sideways glances they gave each other. I kicked a rock. "Does anyone want to come over and hang out?"

Tabby looked like she wanted to, but nervously asked, "Will Brownie be around?"

Tabby and Melanie never did take a liking to my dog. I could sort of see why. Brownie didn't get along with anyone. He tended to be very protective of me, barking and growling at anybody who came near. Since we all lived under the same roof, Dad and Brownie had mutual respect for each other, but still kept a healthy distance. Cyndi couldn't stand Brownie and Brownie couldn't stand her. She had tried to convince my dad to get rid of him once, after Brownie chewed through one of her curtains, but Dad said it saved him money not having to get a security system. If anyone was stupid enough to break in, they got what they deserved. "Nobody would dare rob us after hearing that dog bark," he would say.

"I can make sure Brownie stays down in the basement," I said, trying to reassure her.

I really hated locking him up. He always gave me such a pitifully sad look whenever I did.

"No. That's all right." Tabby tossed her hand. "I really have a lot of reading I should get done today. Timmy said he wants to go out this weekend—" She turned to look at me and her face lit up. "Speaking of which, maybe we can double date with you and Gabe."

My stomach flipped thinking about that. "No way. I like Timmy and all, but I don't think he and Gabe would get along. They're like polar opposites."

"I wish I had a boyfriend," Melanie said.

We looked at her, shocked.

I broke into my best Scarlett O'Hara impression: "Why Melanie Hamilton, you shy thing, you. I've never heard you say anything like that before."

She pushed up her glasses. "I'm a girl."

Tabby and I shot smiles at one another.

"Well, I am," she protested, "and a boyfriend wouldn't be bad."

I stopped and thought about that. It might be just the ticket to pry Melanie out from underneath her parents' domineering thumbs. Mentally, I scrolled through images of Gabe's friends.

We came to the fork in the road. "Well, see you guys tomorrow."

Melanie switched her book bag from one side to the other. "Yeah, see ya."

"See ya, girlfriend." Tabby popped her lip.

I walked the rest of the way home alone.

As I stepped onto my driveway, I heard that same distinct loud motorcycle muffler making another pass as it roared down the main road. I looked around and then went inside.

CHAPTER FIFTEEN

Never Say Never

As I walked through the front door, Brownie moseyed over. "Hi boy." I scratched him behind his crooked ear. Over the last five years, he had grown into a cute, yet regal looking dog.

I held his wide jaw in my hand and made smooch-lips while talking to him in my goofy mommy voice, "And how is my baby?" His stout body flopped to the ground as he turned to jelly. Rolling over, he put his legs straight up in the air. It was his very effective way to get me to rub his tummy. I shook my head. "You are so spoiled." I rubbed his belly.

After he was satisfactorily pampered, he rolled his body, which was all muscle, back over and stood up. "Do you want a treat?" I headed down the hallway. Happily, he followed.

When I passed by my dad's home office, better known as our dining room table, I stopped short. The pile of folders sitting on it was larger than normal. No doubt from all the police activity these last few weeks. Whenever things got super busy at work, he brought his case files home. When I was younger, he'd let me help him by reading off a list of questions the prosecutor planned to ask him on the witness stand. I learned a lot of police procedure listening to his answers.

Impatient, Brownie nudged me forward. "All right, all right." I walked toward the pantry. He trotted up beside me. "Here you go, boy." I pulled out a huge Milk-Bone dog biscuit, the kind he loved, and tossed it high into the air. He jumped up and snagged it in his teeth. Pretending to wrestle with it, he grunted and shook his head back and forth, then pounced down on it and crunched away. Now that I had taken care of my boy, I headed straight to the refrigerator. Scanning the shelves lined with nothing but health crap that Cyndi loved, I moaned in frustration.

Something rustled in the basement garage. I closed the refrigerator door. I heard it again. Then I looked down at the four-legged high-security alarm system lying spread-eagle on the floor as he licked the crumbs from the ground. No way would he be ignoring those noises unless . . . When I turned back around, I saw the book bag dumped near the backdoor and knew who it must be. "You down there, Kylie?" I called out.

"Yeah," my six-year-old sister answered back.

I shook my head. "Where's your mom?"

Kylie yelled up the stairs. "She dropped me off. She said she had to run some errands."

I rolled my eyes. I thought Cyndi was a horrible mother. Lately, she was always "running errands" leaving Kylie home by herself. I wondered sometimes if she even realized she had a daughter, or wanted one. I opened the fridge. "You want something to eat?"

"Nah. I'm fine."

I snagged a yogurt and descended the cellar stairs into the basement garage to see what she was up to.

Kylie was feverishly working, pushing and pulling cardboard boxes like she was a longshoreman. A cute, spunky thing with her brunette hair up in a ponytail, she reminded me of myself at that age. I sat down at the top of the cellar steps. "So how was school?"

"Good."

"Did you learn anything new today?" I pulled the silver foil off the top of the cup and stirred the fruit at the bottom.

"No." She kept her head down, busily going through boxes of toys.

"Nothing?" I asked, skeptical.

She looked up. "Maybe." Her green eyes, that matched mine, flashed wide. "Maybe something about the Pilgrims."

I scooped a bite of yogurt. "The Pilgrims?"

She gave a throw-off wave as she kept her focus on what she was working on. "Yeah, the dudes with the black and white outfits."

I stuffed back a laugh; she slayed me. "Well, what did you learn about them?"

She lifted her head and looked off, deep in thought. "They were pretty cool, starting a new colony and all."

I smiled enjoying the interpretation of history through a six-year-old's eyes.

"Need any help with your homework?"

"Nah. I finished it waiting for mom to pick me up."

Kylie was a whip of a student. I was proud she was my sister. When Cyndi first came on the scene, I hated that my father had married her. I couldn't understand why my sweet dad would have anything to do with someone like that—that was until Kylie was born. Looking back at it now, I'm glad that my dad is such a noble guy.

Kylie started sliding boxes around again, shoving them into the corner.

"What are you doing?"

"Cleaning."

"You're cleaning?" I chuckled. Kylie kept her room like a disaster area.

"Yeah. My mom said she would pay me twenty bucks if I got the garage cleaned out before she got home."

"Twenty bucks!" I shook my head. Cyndi was clueless when it came to money, handing a six-year-old twenty dollars for one chore. Almost every week Fed Ex would arrive at the house with another one of her frivolous purchases. "What are you supposed to clean out?"

She waved her hand around. "The garage, silly."

"Oh . . ." I lowered my head and glanced under the joists. "Why would Cyndi—" My eyes stopped cold on the bare concrete floor. My stomach turned over as I stared in disbelief at the empty spot—the place my mom's car had been parked for the last ten years.

I leaned over and searched out the small windows of the garage doors. "Where's the car?"

"Your mom's?" Kylie slid a toy bucket into the corner. "I don't know."

I tried to remain calm. "It's not in the driveway?"

"No. The truck took it away."

The words struck me like an anvil. Cyndi and I had a fight about this a few days ago . . . but no way would she stoop that low. Vigorously, I shook my head like a boxer who just got nailed by a hook to the head. I stood up and raced down the steps toward the garage door. Lifting it up and over my head, I looked outside, hoping my sister was mistaken.

"How do you know it was taken by a truck?" I asked.

"This morning, when Mom was about to drive me to school, some men were here that Dad had sent over. They towed it away."

I dropped the yogurt. "Dad sent them here?"

"Uh-huh."

"Who told you that? Your mom?"

"No." She paused. "They said it."

I looked at her in disbelief. Bile rose in my throat.

Kylie looked at me and squinted. "Are you okay? You look sort of sick."

My chest heaved up and down in rage. I balled my hands into fists. I wasn't a violent person, but at that moment I wanted to grab a rock and chuck it through a window. Mostly I wanted to knockout my stepmother who had started all this.

"I'm . . ." I tried to hold in the flood of anger that was surging within me. I wanted to run free, so I headed for my old ten-speed bike.

Kylie followed. "Where are you going?"

"I need to get out."

"Simplicity? You're scaring me." She looked at me with concern in her little eyes. "Why don't you wait till Mom gets home?"

I didn't want to leave Kylie, but I knew if Cyndi were here right now, I would start a knockdown drag-out fight with her. "No, I just need to go for a ride. Go back inside."

I frenetically patted Kylie on the arm, trying but failing to reassure her. "I'll be back."

"When?"

I hopped on the bike. "When what?"

Kylie ran along beside me. "When will you be back?"

Overwhelmed with emotion, I shook my head. "Later!" I slammed down on the bike's pedal and sped off down the driveway.

"Simplicity!"

As I raced along, tears began to flow from my eyes. No way would my Dad do that. No way would he just get rid of Mom's car . . . but he had mentioned that it was just there, idle, and then I cut him off before he had time to finish.

I sped down the side street and onto the main road. Tears streamed down so fast I had trouble navigating the thin strip of a breakdown lane, which was covered in sand and trash. A speeding truck blasted its horn. Fear of impending death under a metal fender caused me to overcorrect. As I pulled into the grass, I tried to maintain control of the bike, but it twisted underneath me. The truck horn blared as it narrowly missed me, and then sped by.

Realizing how dangerous this was, I headed toward the access road that led out to the town reservoir. After a mile, I saw the entrance and turned onto it. It was then I heard that same loud motorcycle muffler behind me. I turned and glanced over my shoulder to see a black-helmeted rider following me. As the mug shots of those drug dealers flashed to mind, I pedaled faster. I heard the bike's engine rev higher as it sped up to catch me.

I panicked. Next to the fire gate, partially blocked by large, granite boulders was the entrance to a walking path. I headed for it, hoping the motorcycle was too big to fit through the narrow gap.

I don't know if it was the tears clouding my vision or my fear, but I didn't see the patch of sand. When my bike's tires hit it, they slipped sideways. I frantically squeezed the brakes, but they were useless. I spun out and skidded sideways, straight at the gate. My bike hit the metal bar with a pop, and the impact launched me up and over the handlebars. I twisted through the air like I was rolling down some invisible hill, helpless to stop my rapid descent. My body slammed down onto the asphalt. I slide across the blacktop and then into the grass.

When I came to a stop, my body was shaken.

A second later, I heard the motorcycle come roaring up. My mind screamed *run*, but my body didn't respond. My head foggy, I watched a blurred image of the motorcycle skidding to a stop in front of me. The rider sprang off.

He whipped off his helmet. "Are you all right?"

My tear-soaked eyes had trouble seeing the face, but the voice sounded familiar.

The rider dropped to his knees in front of me, "Simplicity, are you all right?"

Jake. I breathed a sigh of relief.

"Yes, I think so." I looked back at the distance I had tumbled and was amazed. I tried to sit up.

"Don't move. You might've broken something." Anxiously, he scanned my body. "Is your leg hurt?"

I looked down and realized it was twisted awkwardly underneath me, "I don't know."

He looked at it, concerned, "Can I check to see if it's okay?" He put his hands up, "Don't worry, I'll be gentle."

I nodded.

Starting at my thigh, he felt along my leg. The thrilling sensation of his touch, quickly wiped away the fear in my stomach.

He reached my lower leg, "Can you move your foot?"

"I think I can, but my ankle feels funny," I stretched out my toes and it made a weird pop.

He flinched. "That didn't sound too good. Does it hurt?"

"No," I swallowed. "But it doesn't feel right."

"It might be dislocated." He looked toward my arm. "How is your elbow?"

"Fine, I think." I bent it a few times. "Just a little skinned up."

"Anything else hurt?"

I moved my body in a quick wave, checking every major part. "I don't think so."

He nodded, looking relieved.

"The only place that really hurts is my head." I rubbed at my temple. "Man, has it taken a beating this week."

He looked my head over and lightly touched my hair. "I don't see any cuts."

My body started shaking involuntarily.

His expression grew concerned. "Are you cold?"

"No. I think it's more shock than cold."

He whipped off his thick, leather jacket and gently slid it over my shoulders. I squeezed it close as his lingering body heat warmed my quivering body.

"Let me get you out of here." Without hesitation, he slipped one hand under my thighs and the other behind my back and scooped me up in his arms. The sensation of him carrying me, so effortlessly, was exhilarating.

He looked down and smiled, "That was quite a crash."

"Uh-huh." My heart pounded in my chest.

"You scared the crud out of me." He walked back toward my bike.

"I'm sorry I scared you."

He smiled down at me and that adorable dimple popped. "It's okay."

My shoulder felt really good nuzzled into his chest.

"For a spunky, independent thing you sure turn into a damsel in distress easily."

I felt a little embarrassed at the idea that I was helpless. "I'm not a damsel."

He gave me an impish grin, "But you are distressed."

I wanted to swat him, but I was enjoying him carrying me too much.

He stopped and nodded, "I think your bike's totaled."

"Oh, no—my bike." I looked down to see the front wheel bent around the frame. I sighed. "I've had that bike since I was a kid."

"I might be able to fix it."

"What an idiot I was, riding off like that."

"What happened anyway?"

"I lost control."

He looked down at the mangled wreck. "Well, that's obvious." Gently he put me down and leaned me against the gate. Standing directly in front of me, he lifted one sleeve at a time and slipped my arms into the leather jacket, then he zipped me up.

"Better?" He tilted his brow lower.

Keeping my gaze downward, I answered sweetly, "Yes, thank you."

He stepped back and went over to my bike.

I looked around, "Where did you come from anyway?"

"I was just driving by and happened to see you barreling out of your road like a maniac on wheels."

"You did?" I raised an eyebrow. "You just happened to be driving by?"

"Yep."

"My road is like a few miles back."

"I rode slow."

I thought he looked a little guilty, "Slow?"

As I eyed him suspiciously, he kept his gaze downward. "How did you know that's where I lived?"

He froze and didn't respond.

I sighed, "Jake, could you be straight with me, for once?"

"Can you?" he retorted.

I looked him square in the eyes, "This sparring is getting us nowhere."

He glanced off into the woods and shrugged his shoulders, "I don't know. I kinda' like it."

I pointed at his bike, "I heard that motorcycle's muffler a few times this afternoon."

He pressed his tongue into his cheek and gave me the once-over, "What do you want me to tell you?"

"The truth."

"You don't want to hear the truth—people never do."

I challenged him. "Try me."

He stiffened. "I followed your school bus home."

To some girls the revelation would have freaked them out, but for some unknown, thrilling reason it didn't do that to me. The idea that Jake wanted to find out where I lived—excited me more than scared me.

His eyes scanned my face. "Does that upset you?"

"No. It doesn't."

His shoulders relaxed.

"But I don't understand," I shook my head. "The last time we talked, you wanted nothing to do with me."

"Yeah."

"Well, what changed?"

"Gabe."

"Gabe?" I looked at him, puzzled. "What has he got to do with anything?"

He shook his head and then tilted his face down. "Your bicycle's in rough shape," he said changing the subject. "I'll have to come back for it." He slid the bike down the hillside, hiding it in the grass, and then he headed back to his motorcycle. "I think, right now, I need to get you home."

"How?"

He straightened up. "On my motorcycle."

The bike looked old and beat up. There was a license plate, but it was so worn out I could hardly make out the letters. "Where did you get the bike?"

He shook his head. "You ask too many questions."

"You give too few answers."

"Someone gave it to me."

"Is that the truth?"

He looked at me a little shocked. "I've never lied to you."

My face filled with disbelief. "You've never lied to me?"

"No." He shook his head.

I wasn't sure if I should confront him or not, yet. "You sure do hold back tons of information."

"Holding back is what people do. It's hard to trust anyone nowadays." He swung his leg over the seat. "Until people start trusting each other, nothing's ever going to change." He looked up at me. His face as honest and open as a little boy's.

My mind replayed the moment when he jumped off the motorcycle and ran over to me, but this time it wasn't fuzzy. I saw him ripping off his helmet and the concern on his face as he rushed to me. "Jake, do you trust me?"

His tilted his head, "Do you?"

He looked so damn handsome. I felt confused, partly from what I was feeling and partly from our ambiguous conversation. The truth was, I didn't know if I should trust him or not, but I wasn't going to tell him that. I decided to joke instead.

"Do I trust me or you?"

He smiled and shook his head, "Listen, do you want a ride home or not?"

I stared at him.

He looked dejected. "You're hesitating." He knocked back the kickstand. "So you don't trust me."

"No. That's not it." I looked toward the main road. "It's just I don't want to go home right now."

His head rose. "Why not?"

I took in a long deep breath and spit it out, "I'm scared I'm going to beat the tar out of Cyndi."

He looked from left to right. "Who's Cyndi?"

"My jerk of a stepmother."

He chuckled. "Don't hold back your feelings just 'cause I'm here."

"Okay, I won't."

"You're honest, aren't you?"

"Sometimes, to a fault."

He looked down the dirt access road that ran past the fire gate, "So, where were you headed?"

"The reservoir."

He pressed down on the throttle and revved the engine. "Okay. Hop on."

I wavered.

With a Prince Charming like smile, he backed the bike up to me. "Your chariot awaits, m'lady."

My stomach fluttered at the regal compliment. He drew in his shoulder in, enticing me to follow. I fixed my eyes on the walking dark enigma, who straddled a motorcycle wearing black jeans and a black shirt and thought to myself, *I should run.*

I took in a deep breath and inhaled a whiff of the masculine scent that radiated from his leather jacket. Then every single safety precaution my father, my teachers, or anyone else had ever taught me fell silent to the pull I felt.

I hopped on.

CHAPTER SIXTEEN

Walking Disaster

Being with Jake Hanson was like riding a roller coaster—terrifying but exciting.

As we sped down the dirt access road, I was worried I was going to fall off the back, so I clung to him. The old bike had clearly seen better days. It shimmied and jerked along the ruts in the dirt. Every time it bucked, Jake's strong forearms tightened, keeping it under control.

He glanced over his shoulder, and I pointed to the spot where kids would hang out at the top of the dam. He headed in that direction. We rode along the dirt access road that circled the edge of the reservoir, and then onto a walking trail that went up the hill to the backside of the dam. He navigated the bike up the rocky path and then came to a stop at the edge of the woods. Feeling awkward, I immediately hopped off.

He leaned the bike onto the kickstand. "Can you walk?"

I looked down at my foot. "I think so, but then again it still feels weird."

My uncertainty was the only encouragement he needed. He snagged me around the waist and lifted me onto his hip, holding me up under my thighs like I was a kid.

"Umm . . ." Awkwardly, I tried to put my hands—somewhere. As he held me, our faces were inches apart. I pulled my head back, hoping to keep my distance, which was impossible given my position, but still I tried. He made a crooked grin, and then his hands loosened their grip. Thinking I was about to fall, I locked my arms behind his neck and wrapped my legs around his waist. He smiled and impish grin.

I tilted my head and looked at his smug expression. "Hey! Did you do that on purpose?"

"Who, me?" He smiled and pulled me closer.

I swallowed. Feeling his strong muscles wrapped around my body, something deep inside of me uncoiled. I'd never experienced anything like this. I began to understand that there was something unique about a man's body—hard and virile—incredibly different from a girl's yet so absurdly exhilarating. I felt awkward, yet awesome. As an independent-type gal, this was a strange sensation. I had no clue why it was so spine-tingly fantastic to be touched by a man.

He carried me across the top of the dam. "Where would you like to go, Princess?"

The affectionate nickname caused me to blush scarlet. I tried to avoid looking directly at him as I stupidly answered, "Anywhere."

Jake walked us out to the highest point over the dam. Gently, he placed me down. I looked at the sheer fifty-foot drop and trembled. I hated heights. He casually looked around.

"Clearly, you have no fear of heights."

He glanced over the edge and shrugged his shoulders. "Nope."

If it weren't for Jake and the metal railings, I would have backed away, but being near him, gave me a sense of invincibility. I don't' know why, but I felt secure around him. I relaxed a bit and let my feet dangle off the edge while I rested my arms on the lower railing.

Looking down, I watched the deep, blue water churn into white foam as it was sucked into the swirling vortexes near the metal grates. Jake gathered a few stones and started chucking them into the water on the other side of the dam. As my body relaxed, my mind revolted. It bombarded me with all sorts of unanswered questions. I sat for a few minutes, our roles reversed—he appeared relaxed and content, while I fretted.

"You're pretty good handling that bike. Where'd you get it?" I asked again.

"You won't let anything go, will ya?"

"Not unless I get some answers."

"Always wanting the riddles solved."

"The bike?" I asked, unwavering.

He shook his head. "My dad's cousin had it in his shed. After he rolled it and bent the frame, his wife wouldn't let him ride it again, but he never got rid of it. He's letting me use it while I'm here." He bowed slightly as he held out his hands, like he was presenting his story to me.

I thought about it for a second; the explanation made sense. "The bike seems old."

"It is. I tried to fix it, but it's still a little warped."

"So, it's not stolen."

He cocked an eyebrow. "Always thinking the worst, huh?"

"Well, I am a cop's daughter."

"That's for sure." He chucked another rock.

"Where'd you learn how to fix a bike?"

"When we lived off the grid, we had to learn how to do things ourselves. Hunting. Fishing. You name it—we learned it."

"Huh." I said with an uptick to my voice.

Overhead the sound of honking Canadian geese caused us to look up just as the flock, in a V-pattern, flew over us. They circled once and then out onto the lake. In perfect sync, they gracefully transitioned from flyers to mariners as they skimmed the surface.

Jake, leaning on the rail, studied them for a moment. "Exceptional pilots aren't they? I doubt even the Blue Angels could fly in formation as precise."

"The way you talk and carry yourself, I swear sometimes you were in the military."

He smiled as he looked under his shoulder at me. "Close. Military school."

"Oh. I beamed, glad to have another riddle answered.

He stopped watching the geese and went back to the other side where he skimmed the rocks. He threw one nearly perfect; it hopped and skipped playfully over the still, deep water.

"So tell me. What did Gabe want to talk to you about?"

"Oh that . . ." He scratched at the stubble on his chin, rubbing at it hard, like it bothered him. "Xbox."

I gave him a snarky look. "Video games?"

"Yeah." He made a goofy face. "We guys love it."

I wrapped my arms over the lower rail and leaned forward as I placed my forehead on the top bar. "What about Xbox?"

"Gabe offered me his old one." He tossed another rock sidearm. "I would've said no except for my brother."

"Your brother?"

"Yeah. He's still in mourning for his." Jake ran his fingers through his hair. "He's been jonesin' to play again."

"Oh . . ."

He cocked an eyebrow at me. "Nothing sinister in that, is there?"

"I suppose not."

His shoulders were looser and his expression appeared less stark. I couldn't be sure, but I thought he looked almost . . . happy.

"Jake?" I said forcefully.

His head retracted. "Uh-oh. What's coming at me now?" He cocked his head to one side and gave me a dashing smile.

I softened my tone. "You said you never lied to me."

"No." He eyed me cautiously. "I haven't."

Slowly, I said the words, "What about Phoenix?"

He grinned mischievously. "What about it?"

"You lied about living there."

"No, I didn't." He shook his head. "We lived there one summer."

I looked at him in disbelief. "Phoenix?"

"Yes." He made a broad, roguish smile. "Phoenix, Oregon. It's a small city near the northern border of California. My dad got a temp job there one summer as a logger."

"But I asked you if you had hiked the Grand Canyon?"

"Yeah, I've been to the Grand Canyon, once, when I was a kid on vacation."

I sat up straight.

He smirked. "You're the one who jumped to conclusions by putting the two locations together."

I started to think back to my exact wording I used in my interrogation and realized that I had made that mistake. He chuckled and shook his head. "Did you think I was going to tell you where I lived that easily?"

"At the time, I hadn't realized how intelligent you are."

He raised his eyebrows and made a face, no doubt pleased with himself. I shook my head.

His eyes sparkled. "I let you think what you wanted."

"But I'm tired of hearing half-truths," I snapped, more upset with myself than with him.

He stopped and turned to look at me. His expression was solemn. "I've never lied to you Simplicity."

"But what about your past and having to leave your home suddenly, and a million other little riddles," I mumbled.

"Why do you have to know all that stuff?" He shrugged a shoulder. "Can't you just accept me for who I am now?"

I looked up at him. "No. I can't."

His face was sullen as he looked away. "Your choice."

I felt compelled to get to the bottom of this mystery, yet I knew his actions were giant red flags that said stay away, but foolish me had to keep prodding. "So, what secrets are you hiding, Jake?"

"Hiding?" He put his lower arms on the rail and looked off across the lake. Slowly, he opened his fist and the rocks fell from his hand. "Maybe it's the fact that I'm a walking disaster." He tightened his jaw and stared down at the water below.

"Don't all teenager boys think that way?"

He scoffed, "Yeah, I wish I had the troubles of a normal teenager." He scanned the horizon, lost in thought.

I wondered what was going on in his head. "What are you thinking about right now?"

"My brother. He's who I feel for the most. At least I had a few good years. He's never had a normal childhood."

I sighed, feeling for them both.

"Connor's paid a heavy toll," he said.

For a brief instant, he looked vulnerable. Cautiously, I asked, "Is he the only one who's paid that toll?"

"Who else should pay—but me." He stared off into space. "I can handle myself. I'm worried about him. I've always been worried things might get out of hand again and something bad will happen."

"Jake." I took in a deep breath. "Is your father wanted?"

He stopped cold. His hands balled into fists. Silently, I watched an internal struggle play out in his eyes. "Simplicity, you shouldn't ask questions that you don't want to know the answers to."

I swallowed. "I'll take that as a yes."

His brow arched, ominously. Dark Jake was back. "Think what you like."

I didn't know what I was hearing. If his father was wanted, it could be for anything. He could have skipped town for some unpaid parking tickets or been a thief. My dad said once that people run from the police for all sorts of reasons, some rational, some not. One evening my dad had taken me to a community outreach meeting. I sat in the back with a little boy whose curly, black hair and bright eyes still burned in my memory. He and I played while his mom pleaded for help. Her husband was a fugitive from justice. She had put their house up as collateral for his bail. When he skipped town, she lost the house. Now the little boy and his mom had next to nothing, except for each other. My heart sank, thinking something like that was happening to Jake. I could picture him, a boy being dragged from one place to another. Never putting down roots. Never knowing when things might suddenly change. Having no friends. No one who was looking out for him. His harsh exterior and wild ways made more sense now. I could understand as a child having no other choice in the matter to be dragged here or there, but I wondered why, at seventeen, he would keep going on like this. It didn't make any sense. I began to remember something I'd read once. The way Jake acted, brooding and frenetic—I was suspicious about something. "Jake. Does your father ever hit you?"

"No," he snapped. "Why would you say that?" He stepped toward me.

From his body language, I didn't think he was trying to threaten me. He seemed more like a junkyard dog, guarding his fence. I knew that sometimes people who were abused went to great lengths to protect their abusers, so I backed off the subject. "I'm sorry I asked. I didn't mean to offend you. I'm just trying to get to know you better. That's all."

"No, I'm sorry." His posture softened. "I know you didn't mean anything by it." He looked off toward the lake and his voice tempered. " . . . It's just Simplicity, asking her questions."

I watched him as he stared out into the water. I wanted to reach out and help him. I wondered if there were someone he could talk to. I thought about a few of my mom's social worker friends—maybe they could help.

We stayed silent for a few minutes. As the sun began to set behind the pine trees, a beautiful spectrum of oranges and reds filled the sky. I knew I should leave soon, before my dad got home, but I really didn't want this to end. To be honest—I liked being around Jake Hanson.

After a while, he glanced back. "Besides my family, you know more about me than anyone else."

I wanted to say, *I know next to nothing,* but I held my tongue.

He looked at me and his voice and mood lightened. Dropping his shoulders, he smirked. "That must be because you're so good at snooping. Some of the office ladies told me you came in asking a bunch of questions about me."

I raised my head. "Who said that?"

He broke into a wide, devious grin.

"Were you talking with old Mrs. Krueger?" I crossed my arms. "She's always sticking her nose in where it doesn't belong."

"Well, isn't that the pot calling the kettle black." He smiled.

"I was just checking to make sure you weren't a serial jaywalker, that's all."

He laughed. "Oh, is that all? No other reason?"

"Yeah." I lowered my head, hiding my blush. "No other reason."

"I take it back about you being honest."

I squinted. "What do you mean by that?"

"Nothing . . ." He smiled slyly.

"I'm surprised. No one ever gets suspicious when I ask questions." Then I mumbled under my breath, "Up until now. . . . Stupid ladies in the office."

He chuckled.

I looked up at him. "What?"

"They didn't say a word to me."

"They didn't?"

"No . . . I was testing you."

My mouth fell open. "You tricked that out of me?"

He grinned. "Yup."

"Oh, you are clever." I shook my head, pretending I was angry. "I should just leave now."

He raised his chin and turned toward me. "But you won't."

"And how do you know that?"

"One, because then you'd have to walk home."

I looked down at my foot and huffed.

"And two, because there are still way too many questions that you're dying to know the answers to. And that bad boy bait on the end of my lure is much too tempting to walk away from, isn't it?" He rolled a rock in between his finger and thumb.

I squeezed my fist and glared at him at first, but seeing his charming, yet devilish grin, my face quickly broke into a smile. He was right, but I didn't want to say it. I lowered my head and pouted. "It's not just me. Everyone loves a mystery."

He bit his lower lip. "So if the trivial things in my mundane life keep you interested in me, then ask away, future detective."

I laughed. "Trivial and mundane are two words I would never use to describe you."

He began eyeing me intently. The way he looked at me was a little unnerving, yet I couldn't look away. My eyes traveled up and down his attractive build.

He folded his arms. "How would you describe me, then?"

I felt like he had just read my mind. Nervous, I stood up and put my weight against the rail. Then, I went on the offensive. "Why do you dress the way you do?"

He pretended to be insulted as he held out his arms and looked down. "I don't look hot in this outfit?"

I fought back my answer of how incredibly hot he looked.

"You're obviously very intelligent, you don't hang out with the druggies, but you have no clue who the bands are that you're wearing on your shirt. And don't think I can't see you fussing with your long hair and scratching at your stubble like you'd really prefer warningto shave it off."

His eyes grew wide. "Girl, you don't miss much, do you?"

I stretched out my foot and looked down. "Everything except ten-foot-wide gates."

He laughed.

I leaned on my foot a little and it cracked back into place. I cringed, but as I felt the pressure disappear from my ankle, my frown turned into a smile.

He looked down at my foot. "Feel better now?"

I twisted it. "Yeah . . . actually, it does."

"See, there are good reasons for cracking bones."

I beamed, remembering that first day we met, and all those feelings I started to have sitting on his lap in the car. He smiled back over his shoulder at me. Now that he was finally opening up, I realized that behind the steel façade was a warm, charismatic young man.

I pressed on my foot, testing it out. "So is that all you and Gabe talked about at lunch?" I was fishing for some more answers—of a different sort now.

"No." He threw a rock hard—like a bullet—out across the water. "He told me you two were dating now."

My stomach flipped in nervousness. I realized he was carefully watching my reaction. I kept my head down. I don't know why I felt like I shouldn't be discussing this with him, as if I was guilty or something. "We're going out for dinner tomorrow night—that's all." I picked up a pebble and tossed it out over the water.

"That's all?" He grunted, and then pitched another rock high in the air.

I watched him for a minute. His shoulders were rigid and his jaw had tightened. He ran both his hands through his hair.

"So Jake. Why this one-eighty?"

"What one-eighty?"

"Following me home? Hanging out with me now?"

"I don't know."

He shrugged his shoulders as if he didn't care, but I could tell he did. "You don't know why?"

He cast a sideways glance. "Maybe I do—but I'm not about to tell you."

I snickered, "Are you chicken?"

He raised an eyebrow. "You do know how to push my buttons, don't you?"

"Who, me?" I teased.

He huffed. I leaned away and covered my mouth with my fist as I made a little "balk-balk" sound like a chicken.

He stood up straight, smiled wide, and turned to stand directly in front of me. His masculine stance and close proximity unsettled something deep within me. I stared up into his devastatingly handsome face, and then, I promptly hiccupped.

He laughed. "Never took you for a belcher."

"Excuse me?" I covered my mouth. "That was a hiccup."

"If you say so," he jested.

Embarrassed, I tried to lower my gaze but he kept staring into my eyes. I couldn't look away; he had an intoxicating effect on my brain.

"One of us should speak," I said.

"Don't look to me. I'm not good at opening up."

I sighed.

He shrugged his shoulders.

"Jake." I lowered my head and spoke toward the ground. "Would you open up . . . for me?"

When I glanced up at him, his face had transformed. His expression looked like a little boy, innocent yet, scared. He took in a long, deep breath and then plunged in. "I'm jealous. That's why I followed you home, and that's why I'm here now."

My heart fluttered from the frank declaration. "Why would you be jealous? I thought you hated me. You made it abundantly clear you didn't even want to be my friend."

He swallowed hard. "I didn't think you should be friends with me—not that I didn't want to be near you."

A thrill ran unhindered inside me. Could this sweet, hunky—but seriously messed up boy—really like me?

My mind screamed a warning: Danger! Do not fall! I knew he was holding something back from his past, something serious, but I didn't know what it was. The way I was feeling about him right now—that giant unanswered riddle—frightened me. My head spun trying to decide what to do. I stepped back toward the rail and my fear of heights kicked in. I squeezed the metal bar trying to stay upright.

He reached out to steady me. I looked down at his hand on my waist. The concern he kept showing via his actions weren't those of an evil person. He was noble.

I blurted out, "I like you, Jake."

He pulled back. "Simplicity, I don't think we should get close."

I looked at his brown, brooding eyes adrift in pain, and my heart sank. His damaged aura drew me in—like metal to a magnet. "My brain is telling me we shouldn't either." I nodded. "So I have decided to stop thinking."

He chuckled. "Why can't I drive you away?"

I put my hand on his arm. "Because I see something in you…something good."

He clenched his jaw. "Things I've done in the past most people would never forgive."

Nervously, I swallowed.

He shook his head. "I like you to, but I don't want to see you get hurt."

I squeezed the railing. "I don't think you'll hurt me."

He anxiously looked around. "I don't know how long I'm going to be here. It could be a day or a week."

He was trying his best to ward me off, but it was too late. I had jumped off the cliff and fallen for him—hard. "I don't care, Jake Hanson."

He raised his hand to my cheek and stroked it with his thumb. "I'm sorry how I've been acting. Pushing you away." His touch was soft and gentle. "Believe me, it's not what I wanted."

"I'm sorry I wouldn't take, *get lost*, for an answer."

He smiled. "I'm really glad you didn't."

As I became captivated by his eyes, my head spun. His tanned skin and manly scent stirred feelings in me. I imagined my hands sliding into his hair as it ran in between my fingers. His warm breath caressed my skin. I couldn't stop gazing at his lips as I daydreamed about them pressing down onto mine.

His eyes softened. "You know what it'll mean if we take this step?"

My chest heaved. "What?"

Softly he spoke. "I'm never going to forget you."

My body unraveled and I nearly fell back over the railing. I felt something deeply profound that I had never felt before with any of the boys I'd casually dated. They liked me—but Jake wanted me.

"Please don't ever forget me, Jake, because I'm *never* going to forget you."

He slid his hands into my hair as he tilted my head. Leaning towards me, he inched his lips closer. I squeezed the metal bar, trying to stop my hands from shaking. Then, gently, he pressed his lips onto mine. My heart raced as the heady sensation of my first kiss spun me into a magical world.

The feeling of his lips—warm and soft—was more than I could handle. The little girl inside of me giggled and ran in circles as out surged the feelings of a woman. I let go of the railing and reached out for him. Sliding my arms up his chest, I felt the hearth-like warmth under my fingertips.

He unzipped the leather jacket and slid his hands along my waist. Then he gently stroked my back. His rough fingers penetrated through the fabric as his touch sent shivers of pure elation racing across my skin.

"You can't imagine how incredible you feel," he whispered. My head reeled, as I felt him cocoon me in his tender touch. As our bodies pressed together, we kissed again. I slid my hands around his waist, grabbed a clump of his shirt and pulled him closer. He moaned as a flood of overwhelming sensations whirled inside my body.

"Jake," I murmured. His mouth responded, and our kisses quickly intensified.

My body seemed to be splitting in two, as dormant parts of me broke forth in longing. I'd never felt this way—desired, secure and *oh, so alive.*

Invincible in each other's arms, we melted together.

His amazing kisses, easy and tender, made me feel like I was soaring to the gates of heaven. Heatedly, we kissed until we became so overwhelmed we had to stop to catch our breath.

He wrapped his arms around me. "I've never been this close to anyone. Ever."

"Neither have I."

As we held each other, I rested my cheek on his chest. He took a deep breath, inhaling the scent of my hair, and then placed his chin gently on the crown of my head.

As darkness began to descend, we became oblivious to everything else in the world.

After a few minutes, he pulled back and tenderly cupped my face in his hands. "Simplicity," he gazed into my eyes, "I'm worried that when you learn about my past, you'll want nothing to do with me."

I looked up into his soft, warm eyes. The genuine affection I saw reflected in his gaze, made my heart soar. "Oh, Jake. I was wrong. Whatever mistakes you've made in the past are done. Only the here and now matters. And at this moment, nothing you ever say will drive me away from you."

He looked at me still unsure. I pulled him in and kissed him. We savored the moment we knew we'd never forget. Everything that had led up to this moment now seemed like providence, as if this was always meant to be. We kissed for a while longer, just soaking each other in.

Then, suddenly, in the distance a set of bright headlights came speeding up the access road. The vehicle screeched to a halt at the fire gate.

Jake turned to look. "Who could that be?"

I had to squint to see. The car stopped for a moment, then the gate flew open and the car sped down the restricted access road.

I panicked. "Oh, no! I hope it's not . . ."

Only two groups of people had the keys to that gate. One was the fire department. The other was the police.

Frantically, I asked, "Is it a police cruiser?"

Jake narrowed his eyes and stared for a second at the speeding car. Then his hand went around my waist. He slid me behind his body, shielding me. He shook his head.

"No. That's not a cop car."

To be continued . . .

Dear Reader,

I am *so* sorry to have to stop here, but it's the best place. The story demands it!

Thank you very much for reading my book. Life for so many of us is hard, but good stories have a way of easing our burden. These characters have come alive because you've read them bringing them to life. So many others out there need a pick-me-up—a glimmer of hope at the end of a long, hard day. If you like this story, I hope you will tell others about it.

My website is Katherine-Greyson.com. I love giving things away. If you sign up for my newsletter, you'll automatically be entered in a contest to win a brand new HD Fire Kindle Tablet. In addition, I'll send you advanced notice of *Everyone Keeps Secrets—Book Three, Hidden Pasts*. Also, I plan in the near future to add tons of other great things to the site like background stories and trivia about the characters.

If you're craving another good story, you should check out my husband's novels. His high-octane mystery series featuring rogue police officer Jack Stratton is out of this world. Here is the link to all his bestselling books: Christopher-Greyson.com

I really appreciate all the wonderful emails you have sent, encouraging me to keep writing. I especially love to see how many of you have told others about the story. It truly warms my heart. So feel free to stop by and drop me an email.

With Love,
Katherine Greyson

www.Katherine-Greyson.com

The story continues
in
Volume Three
"Hidden Pasts"

We turn our attention to Jake's mother, Isabella Crawford, and her mottled past. While Simplicity begins the hunt to learn more of Jake's troubles.

Please look for the book:
Hidden Pasts

Then the series continues
Volume 4: *The Return*
All the threads of the tapestry begin to weave together.
Volume 5: *Resolution*
The final climactic conclusion to our saga.

Please don't forget to go to <u>Katherine-Greyson.com</u> to sign up for updates on new book releases as well as enjoy free items and giveaways.

www.Katherine-Greyson.com

Acknowledgments

I would like to thank the best content editor my husband, Christopher Greyson. He is not only an unbelievably supportive husband he is also a great author and I am so grateful for his help and most importantly his unconditional love.

To my wonderful children who helped me in so many ways. I wish all mothers had the joy of such caring, brilliant kids as you. I can't wait for your books to be published. You go guys!

I would like to thank Faith Williams for helping me to refine the prose. To Stephanie Handy for her tireless efforts line editing. To Karen Lawson and Janet Hitchcock for their hard work and dedication copy editing these books. I am forever grateful to you all and blessed to have found such fine editors.

My thanks and appreciations go out to all those wonderful beta readers who helped me hone this story. You are wonderful.

Last, but not least, I want to thank YOU for picking up this book and bringing these characters to life. If it weren't for your support, Simplicity, Jake, and all the wonderful cast of characters would not be here. Thank you! Thank you! Thank you!

Ordering Information:

Quantity sales. Special discounts are available on quantity purchases by corporations, associations, and others. For details, contact the "Special Sales Department" at the web address above.

27415725R00125

Made in the USA
San Bernardino, CA
12 December 2015